I0664242

Bless Your Heart

WANDA JENNINGS

BOOK NINE OF THE MAGNOLIA MANOR SERIES

Printed in the United States of America
First Printed September 2025

Published by:
Between Friends Publishing,
1080 GA Hwy 96, Suite #100,
Warner Robins, Georgia 31088

ISBN: 978-1-956544-73-2

*This book is dedicated to my cousin Tyler,
his father Waylon who fought in Vietnam,
and to my grandmother who adored them
both.*

Chapter One

"You can't baptize that baby in winter," Maude shook her head. "She'll freeze slam to death."

"It's not technically winter," Opal countered. She launched into an explanation of how the seasons were originally named and which months of the year fell into which season according to the calendar.

"I don't care what season April is in," Maude shrugged. "It's colder than a frosted frog out here."

"What exactly does that even mean?" Ruby giggled from the pew ahead of her. She had opened her Bible to a random passage and had been trying to read to pass the time, but she kept getting distracted.

"Well, I was going to say it's colder than a witch's tit, but I knew you'd get all up in arms about that one," Maude smirked.

"Maude! Shh," Ruby hissed. She had gone beet red and sank down in the pew. Maude never failed to embarrass her when people were around. The small church was filled with her neighbors and fellow Rhinestonians that were waiting for Brother George Barton to walk up to the pulpit. He had gotten caught at the back of the aisle by the organ player, Tammy, who was complaining about the songs the choir director had chosen for the week. Tammy preferred a more consistent song list that didn't vary from week to week, but Brother Barton had left the song list up to the choir director, Thurmond Decater, much to Tammy's fury.

"Who decided how cold that is exactly?" Opal pondered. Before either she or Maude could further reveal their thoughts on the subject, Ruby turned around and shushed them again. Somehow Barton had managed to break away from Tammy's tirade and rushed to the pulpit before she could start again. Tammy begrudgingly stomped to the ancient organ and began playing the call to worship. The Sunday morning church service was about to begin.

Maude Cooper and Opal Tyler sat behind the Montgomery family made up of Ruby, her husband Jameson, and their ten year-old-daughter Melanie every Sunday at Beaver Crossing Holy Church for the Faithful. Jameson was one of the deacons and though he tried to keep a straight face during the conversation, even he couldn't hide the fact that Maude and Opal's hilarity had tickled him. He playfully shook his head at Melanie who had turned around to giggle at the two women behind her. Opal winked at the young girl and then pulled out the hymnal from the back of the pew in front of her so she could sing along to the opening song that the choir had begun to sing.

Opal's voice carried loudly over the crowd. The new choir director had been begging Opal to join the choir for the past six weeks, but Opal was playing hard to get. She had the voice of an angel, but she wasn't too keen on giving up her Wednesday evenings for choir practice. She preferred to spend her Wednesday evenings in Junction at the VA playing bingo. She was generally the youngest person there by far, but she always had a blast. At thirty-two she was in her prime, according to all of the World War II veterans who always showed up on Wednesdays for bingo night. They could occasionally talk her into coming to one of their dance nights where they entertained each other with old war stories and attempts at ballroom dancing. On a good night, she would drag Maude with her and they'd dance the night away with gentlemen in their seventies who could still keep time with the music.

The VA was where she had first signed up for the pen pal program. A nearby chapter in Birmingham had begun collecting letters and donations for soldiers in Vietnam, and Opal readily signed up. The object was to establish a friendly relationship with a soldier overseas and write them letters frequently in an effort to boost morale, but Opal decided that she would rather write to many of the young men over there instead of just one. She always kept her letters jovial and filled them in on the latest celebrity gossip, baseball scores, and the ins and outs of life in a small town. It pained her any time she received a letter marked return to sender or got wind of news that one of her pals had been killed or was reported missing. Even though she did not technically know any of these men from Adam, she couldn't help but feel a mixture of anger and sadness for their untimely demise. She had never met any of these men in person, but she felt a spiritual connection to each one. She refused to watch anything on the news channels. The faceless voices sometimes haunted her at night after she received bad news regarding one of her own pals. Maude told her she could find a way to support the war effort elsewhere, but Opal knew she couldn't give up. The men needed tokens of home, even if they were written in the impeccable handwriting of a pixie like woman. Her letters meant the world to these men. Especially to one in particular, her favorite cousin, Thomas Eugene West, a combat medic from outside of Memphis. Opal and Thomas hadn't seen each other since they were teenagers, but one serendipitous moment changed that. He was on leave visiting his parents and she was returning from one of her adventures as a speaker at a hair care and makeup convention in Nashville. As fate would have it, he sat next to her and they chatted all the way to Montgomery where they both got off the train. Opal believed in both fate and divine intervention. She had been reunited with one of her childhood best friends and closest family members. They wrote to each other weekly. Opal always offered for Maude to read the letters Thomas sent her, but the mere mention of blood and jungle snakes turned Maude a pale shade of green and she begged Opal to skip over those parts.

The war wasn't pretty. The nightly television programs showed more carnage and grisly reports than ever before. Morale both overseas and at home was tanking, but still in the spring of 1971, the draft raged on. More and more men, young and old, were sent packing to the faraway jungle. No town in the state hadn't been ravaged by the mile long lists of names that echoed the missing and killed. Some of Rhinestone's finest had come back in pine boxes and were interred at Deer Lane Cemetery not too far from the grounds of Beaver Crossing. There had been too many funerals and wailing mothers and widows over the past few years. There were even a few empty seats in the pews at Beaver Crossing every Sunday morning.

After the choir sang their songs, Brother Barton gave an impassioned sermon on the concept of forgiveness. Once he bowed his head and prayed one last time, Tammy banged on the organ keys to signal the end of the service. Jameson followed the rest of the deacons to the front pew for their monthly meeting while Ruby, Melanie, Maude, and Opal walked outside and stood underneath the tallest cypress tree by the riverbank to talk. Nadine Waters and her group of friends could be heard arguing about something nearby. Nadine gestured wildly and pointed at the front of the church and then over by the cluster of trees.

"What's she saying?" Maude asked. She craned her neck to try and decipher what Nadine was all up in arms over.

"How do I know?" Opal shrugged. "Why don't you go and ask her? I'm sure she'd love to tell you!"

Maude rolled her eyes and sighed loudly. "That woman is the bane of my existence." As much as she was dying to know who or what Nadine was gossiping about, she didn't have it in her to walk the ten yards over to her to find out.

"Hello Nadine!" Ruby called out suddenly. Nadine instantly perked up and waved for the small group of women who surrounded her to follow her over to where Ruby was standing. "Hello Ruby. Hello precious," Nadine smiled at Melanie. "And Opal, you really should reconsider Mr. Thurman's request to join the choir. We have such a lovely time making a joyful noise for the Lord."

Maude choked on the salted peanuts she had found while rummaging around in her purse. Ruby whacked her on the back which sent bits of the snack flying. "And there you are," Nadine smirked. "I thought I heard you singing this morning. I knew it was either you or a screech owl that got loose in the rafters again."

Maude's fist tightened at her side but Ruby quickly changed the subject. "Sure was a lovely service today," she smiled. "Forgiveness is for everyone."

"Yes, it was," Nadine agreed. "And congratulations, Melanie, for making the decision to get baptized next month. I can't wait to see it."

"It's going to be cold," Maude whispered.

"Well, as much as I'd like to disagree, she is right," Nadine nodded. She gagged slightly at the thought of agreeing with Maude Cooper, but the uncouth woman standing before her was right. "We've got to figure out something better than an old cow trough for baptisms." She sighed disdainfully over to her right where the area for baptisms had been designated.

Beaver Crossing had been using a concrete cow trough that the deacons had dug a pit in the ground for and secured in the dirt for the past few years. It wasn't the ideal situation, but it was what they had. Being a country church had its charm, but a steel hole in the ground wasn't one of them. Especially when the temperature was still low enough to require a jacket or shawl before and after the service. The summer months were better for outdoor baptisms, but even then the flies, mosquitoes, and the threat of an errant alligator from the swampy creek was enough to make the pastor want to sprinkle the person's forehead versus a show of full on submersion.

This wasn't the first time that someone had brought up the impracticality of an outdoor baptismal, but the church couldn't afford to set aside funds for anything indoor. The deacons had tried taking up special collections and fundraisers before, but something else always needed fixing when it came down to it. The paint was peeling, the carpet aisle was molding, and the designated fellowship hall couldn't hold more than ten people at a time.

"We're just going to have to do something about it ourselves," Nadine quipped.

"Do something?" Patsy Collins inquired. "About what?"

"We need a proper baptismal," Nadine explained. "We've needed one for years and it's past time for waiting. It's time we do something."

She waved her hands around and pointed at each of the women standing together.

"Like what?" Maude asked. Her interest was piqued, even if it was Nadine taking charge.

"We need to form some sort of committee to spearhead this," Nadine said. "To take over and get things moving."

"Sounds expensive," Ruby frowned.

"Which is why we need a fundraiser," Nadine nodded. "The likes of one this town has never seen." She looked around at the faces staring back at her. "No more waiting on the men to run things, it's time we take charge and get what we need."

"We need a cool name for this squad," Opal mused.

"Squad?" Maude asked.

"Not like a cheer squad," Opal chuckled.

"I know that," Maude hissed.

"A squad like an epic band. Every great girl band has a cool name," Opal pointed out. "The Supremes, The Pointer Sisters, The Ronettes. So many good ones."

"She has a point," Maude nodded. She chewed on the end of the candy bar wrapper and ripped it open with her teeth. She took a big bite of the caramel and chocolate bar and smacked her lips. "The Andrews Sisters, too."

"The Beach Boys, The Beatles," Ruby interjected happily. "The Monkees, oh! The Jackson Five!"

"I didn't know this was a competition," Maude smirked.

"I said girl bands," Opal clarified. "Nadine

said she couldn't wait for the men anymore, so I assume she wants an all-girl band."

"Not a band," Nadine said. "More like a team. Some sort of committee, a chamber, a commission to get things done."

"To serve and protect!" Opal cheered.

"No," Nadine laughed. "To get things done around here."

"Around here?" Patsy asked.

"Here at the church and around town," Nadine explained. "Rhinestone deserves our tenacity."

"We still need a name," Opal shrugged.

"The Super Squad," Patsy offered.

"None of us have super powers," Maude countered.

"Speak for yourself," Opal whispered.

"The Church Posse," Lulu McBride chimed in.

"Sounds too manly," Belle Wilbanks frowned. "What about the Sisters!"

"We aren't nuns," Ellen Abernathy shook her head.

"Plus we've already got a copyright on that sort of name," Opal winked at Maude and Ruby.

Maude, Ruby, and Opal had long been nicknamed the Stone Sisters after their cherished lifelong friendship and in honor of their beloved town where they all grew up. It didn't hurt that Ruby and Opal also shared their names with precious gemstones.

"Yea, none of us are nuns," Maude hiccupped.

"It needs to be something edgy," Opal mused. "Something catchy and memorable, unless this is a one off type thing."

"I think it could certainly become something bigger," Nadine said. She was suddenly drunk with the idea of revolution and positive change. There was a laundry list of projects that came to mind and she would be the one to bring it all to fruition.

"The Roller Girls," Lucille said. "Because we're on a roll! Get it?"

"Makes it sound like we are on a roller skating team," Ruby giggled.

"The Ladies Auxiliary," Nadine gasped.

"I like it," Ruby smiled. "The Ladies Auxiliary."

"I've heard better," Opal said. "But it does have a nice ring to it."

"So, are you all in?" Nadine asked.

"Yes," all the women but Maude squealed.

"Maude?" Nadine asked.

"I'm good," Maude said, swallowing the last bite of chocolate.

"She's upset it's not a band," Opal said. "She's been wanting to pick up the guitar, but sadly no band will take her on. This was her last chance."

"What?" Ruby giggled.

"Oh hush!" Maude hissed.

"Well, suit yourself," Nadine shrugged. "Alright ladies, this is it. The Ladies Auxiliary is officially, well, it's officially formed. Let's do this!"

"What are we doing again?" Belle asked.

"First things first," Nadine answered unwaveringly. "It's time to brainstorm the best fundraiser Rhinestone has ever seen."

"And what exactly would that be?" Maude asked.

"I don't know now, but when I do, I'll let you

know!" Nadine said. She turned on her heel and practically flew to her car. They all watched her disappear in a cloud of dust down the dirt road.

"Well that was completely unnecessary," Maude coughed.

"She's a loose cannon, but she's got style," Opal laughed.

Chapter Two

An hour later, the Montgomery family sat around the table at their favorite local buffet after Jameson's meeting at church had finished. Maude and Opal joined them and they caught Jameson up on Nadine's grand idea. Jameson truly believed that it was a good thing. The church and other foundations in Rhinestone needed help, and he was simply too busy to dedicate any more time than what he already had. Most of his friends who were also deacons were too busy to put any more time or effort into the growing list of projects either. After listening to them explain Nadine's thought process, he asked Maude why she wasn't so keen on joining the rest of the women in this new endeavor, but she merely scoffed. It wasn't that she didn't think it was a good idea; she would be happy to donate money and allow that to be her contribution. She had never been one who wanted to spend time sitting around a table gossiping. She knew at the end of the day that it could be a good idea, but she didn't necessarily trust Nadine to be the one to spearhead it. She and Nadine had a long history of being what many referred to as frenemies. It had all started when they were young teenagers. No one could pinpoint when exactly it started, but the two women had never been bosom buddies. Maude would never admit that she and Nadine both seemed to enjoy their little spats, even if it did annoy everyone around them.

"I really do think it's a great idea," Jameson said. He added another dash of pepper to his mashed potatoes and took another sip of his sweet tea. He was looking forward to a thick slice of chocolate cake that Betsy had just put out behind the counter of the dessert line. If he didn't hurry, he might not get a piece. Betsy's cakes were always in high demand and he didn't want to miss out on one.

"You do?" Maude asked. She eyed Jameson warily and grabbed a roll from the basket in the center of the table and slathered butter on it.

"I agree with what Opal said. Sometimes you have to do things yourself," he nodded. He swallowed the last bit of mashed potatoes and asked if anyone else wanted anything from the dessert counter.

Maude had already piled her plate high with two pieces of pecan pie. Melanie stood up and said that she would walk with him to get a piece of cake. He asked Ruby and Opal if they wanted anything but they both shook their heads. Ruby was still working on her fried chicken and Opal had already launched into an explanation about work ethic.

"I got that from Ms. Belva," Opal explained as she crunched on a rather firm carrot from the salad bar. "She's always been firm on that notion. If you want to see something done right, she said it's best to do it yourself. That philosophy has worked wonders for her."

Belva Sinclair was the proud founder, owner, and operator of the Comb Over Salon, the premier salon and spa in Rhinestone. She had been the first female business owner to open up in town, and she was without a doubt the most successful business owner, male or female, in this part of the state. Opal had worked with her for the past ten years and was hoping to one day take over the salon when Belva retired. The salon was the perfect place for a free spirit like Opal who could never see herself working in a mechanic's garage or a classroom like her two best friends, Maude and Ruby.

Maude Cooper had worked with her father at his family's garage for as long as she could remember. She loved the smell of gasoline and grease and could tell anyone who cared to listen more about engines and carburetors than any man in town. Her knowledge came in handy whenever someone's car or lawnmower needed fixing. She had recently bought a house with some land next door to Opal's great-aunt Wilhelmina who owned twenty acres just past the highway. No one knew for sure how old Aunt Willy was. Willy was known to disappear for weeks on end, though she always returned with a new treasure trove of fascinating objects, herbs, and stories. She had vowed to never retire, even though no one was quite sure what exactly she did for a living, but when she offered to sell Opal ten of the acres that had a beautiful house on the plot, Opal knew she couldn't pass up that deal. She had moved in two months ago and was already redecorating the bungalow to her own specifications and likes. Opal and Maude were neighbors, which greatly pleased them both.

Ruby had been the only one of the three friends who took the more traditional route after college. The summer after she received her teaching degree, she set off on an epic vacation with Maude and Opal. On the trip she found out she was pregnant with Melanie. Once she returned to Rhinestone, she and Jameson decided to elope. When Melanie was a toddler, Ruby decided to put her degree to good use and got a job at the elementary school. She loved teaching at Rhinestone Elementary, the same school she had first met Maude and Opal at many decades ago. The elementary school connected to the middle and high school where they all shared a rather large gymnasium that doubled as the auditorium for special events. Ruby loved being at the same school as her daughter Melanie for the past few years and wasn't looking forward to her being in the middle grades building next door. Time was flying far too quickly as her only child continued to grow. She and Jameson had always planned on having more children, but for whatever reason, it wasn't to be. Melanie was more than enough and they were ever so thankful for her good health and vivacious spirit. Jameson often remarked that they couldn't have planned out a better life than the one they had.

Melanie was a bright and gifted child. She took after both her mother and father in that regard. She always did well in school and never struggled to make friends. She had Jameson's extroverted personality and Ruby's bookish intelligence. Depending on the day, she wanted to grow up to be a teacher, an astronaut, or a famous actress. Jameson and Ruby always told her that she could be anything she wanted to be if she put her mind to it. Growing up with Maude and Opal as her surrogate aunts furthered that belief in herself. Opal had taken her to Montgomery one weekend where they spent the evening at the local performing arts theatre. Melanie had not stopped talking about lights, the sounds, and the beautiful actresses in their costumes all these weeks later. She had been bitten by the acting bug!

"I agree," Ruby said after Opal had launched into another story involving Ms. Belva. "There's nothing that says we can't find a way to get things done."

"Absolutely," Jameson agreed. He and Melanie had returned from the dessert bar with an extra-large piece of cake each. Ruby wasn't sure how in the world he had room after eating all of that fried chicken, mashed potatoes, green beans, and corn soufflé, but she knew better than anyone that Jameson Montgomery had a sweet tooth.

"Y'all know that Nadine won't stop there," Maude said. "She's like a dog on a bone. Once you get her going, she won't stop. Might be good for the old place to get a new look," she mused. She saw the look of surprise on Ruby's face and quickly added, "but don't tell her I said that!"

"She'd never believe it anyway," Ruby smiled.

"Beaver Crossing is about to enter the next century," Jameson chuckled. "It's about time."

"Who says women can't lead!" Opal cheered.

"I couldn't help but overhear your spirited conversation," a voice interrupted.

"And who are you exactly?" Maude asked. The man at the table next to theirs tipped his hat and introduced himself as Andy Jenkins. He said he was in town on business and couldn't help but overhear what they had been talking about.

"Where I come from, women keep their pretty little hands out of a man's business," he drawled.

"A man's business?" Maude asked sharply.

"Well, the way I see it, the church is a man's business. The Lord himself is a man," Andy continued.

"Pretty little hands? Has he seen Maude's hands?" Opal whispered to Ruby.

"I think he's about to," Ruby whispered back.

They watched as Maude threw down her napkin and turned all the way around in her chair to face the burly man. "First of all, I don't remember any of us asking for your permission about what we involve our hands in. Secondly, the church is for anyone. And third of all, these women in this town could teach you a few things!"

Andy raised his eyebrows and chuckled to himself. He craned his neck to look past Maude at Jameson. "This here your woman?"

Jameson took his glasses off and cleaned them with a handkerchief from his pocket. He was not keen on getting involved with this stranger, and he knew that the women were able to take care of things themselves. "My woman?" Jameson asked.

"Yea. Which one of them belongs to you?" Andy asked.

"None of these women here are property. If you're asking if she's my wife, then no. Is there something else you need, Mr. Jenkins?" Jameson asked calmly, but sternly. All he wanted was to finish his cake and then go home and take one of those good Sunday after church naps.

"Oh no, I just couldn't believe that women were discussing business matters of all things," Andy said.

"Everyone has a right to talk about whatever they like. Now if you don't mind, we'd like to get back to our meal," Jameson said curtly.

"Interesting," Andy continued to grin. His eyes flickered over Ruby and Opal who had been fairly quiet during this interchange.

"What exactly is so interesting?" Maude snapped.

"Oh nothing," Andy snickered. He picked up his fork and went back to eating his fried pork chop.

"The nerve of some people," Maude hissed. Her cheeks were red and they could all see that her dander was up. It wasn't hard to get Maude riled up, but this strange man succeeded quicker than most.

In an obvious effort to change the subject, Opal turned to Melanie and smiled. "Well, Melanie, how did your first meeting go this week?"

Melanie had decided to join the Girl Scouts and had her first meeting a few days ago. "It was so much fun! There's so much to learn. I got my uniform!" Melanie was tickled pink at the thought of her new adventures.

"That sure is interesting," Maude nodded. She was doing her best to calm down and finish her dessert. The pie really was delicious. The extra whipped cream she had smothered the piece of pie in only made it better. "Betsy makes some real good pie," she said in between mouthfuls. "I wish I could bake like she does."

The man behind her snorted and didn't even try to hide his derision.

"What on earth is so funny?" Maude demanded.

"Nothing," Andy smirked. "I just find it interesting that three grown women are out to lunch with this fine gentleman here. I thought families were supposed to have home-cooked meals on Sunday? That's how we do it back in my town," Andy shrugged.

"Why don't you go back to your town then," Maude seethed.

"Yes, back home the women stay quiet and knit and cook. They don't speak unless they are spoken to. Y'all do things mighty different around here," Andy said ignoring the furious stares from the nearby tables. He was gathering quite the interest from the families of Rhinestone that were eating at nearby tables.

Maude clinched her fist and bit her tongue. Ruby was too shocked to say anything. She scooted closer to Melanie who was in between her and Opal watching the scene unfold. "Just ignore him," Jameson said. He had reached his limit from this man, but he also knew that men like Andy enjoyed causing a scene and it would be best to ignore him and let him fizzle out.

"Be a good girl and turn back around," Andy said. "The men are talking."

"I have nothing to say to you," Jameson said directly. He could feel his cheeks redden. It was not often that he got angry, but this stranger was the height of rudeness.

Maude turned around and stabbed the last bite of pecan pie and shoved it in her mouth. She chewed with a ferocity that had everyone around the table watching to see what she did next. Andy was still staring at the back of her head with an evil grin on his face.

"I remember a time when restaurants didn't allow women unless they were in the kitchen cooking," Andy continued.

Opal got a devious smirk on her face and said, "well that's showing your age. They even let us vote now."

"Can't say that I agree with that one either," Andy said.

"Who hurt you?" Maude asked. She had had just enough of this overbearing man to last her a lifetime. "Because I doubt any woman in your life willingly puts up with you. You have single-handedly ruined our lunch and the lunch of anyone in this vicinity."

"You can't talk to me like that," Andy said. He stood up and smoothed out the sleeves of his jacket.

"I'll talk to you however the hell I want to," Maude sassed back. She turned to her friends at the table and shook her head. "I'm so mad I can't even eat. I'm going for a ride. I'll see you later!"

"Be careful," Ruby called out. "Don't wreck your bike on account of this, well, man."

"Bike?" Andy stuttered. "You don't mean that she rides a motorcycle?"

"I sure the hell do!" Maude snapped. "And I know for a fact it's too much for you to handle!" She stomped out of the restaurant and sped away leaving Andy with his mouth agape.

"I think it's time you followed suit and went back to whatever planet you're from," Opal said plainly. "Goodbye Andy. Don't let the door hit you where the good Lord split you."

Before Andy could utter another word, the waitress who had witnessed everything snatched his plate and drinking glass and cleaned the table. Betsy, the owner's wife, had come around from behind the dessert counter and took his chair and the extra chair from his table leaving him nowhere to sit.

Jameson didn't hide the big smile that had spread across his lips. Men like Andy gave his gender a bad name and it was nice to see that behavior like that would never be tolerated in his hometown, the best small town this side of the Mississippi.

"I'm surprised she didn't throw that glass of sweet tea in his face," Jameson chuckled.

"Maude's a lady," Ruby shook her head.

"No she's not," Opal laughed. "She just loves tea too much to spill it."

Chapter Three

Nadine's groundbreaking idea spread through the town of Rhinestone like a wildfire. Everyone was gung ho for the idea! Nadine called for a meeting of any like-minded women to gather for the first official meeting. The only problem was finding somewhere that would house such a meeting. Ruby quickly volunteered her home, Magnolia Manor, as the host spot. She pestered Jameson and Melanie for days until she was satisfied that the Manor was polished and shiny enough to entertain some of the finest women in Rhinestone. She was sure that her floors had never been cleaner. She had even made sure that Melanie's room was the cleanest it had been in years, even if no one would be going upstairs.

Magnolia Manor was one of the loveliest homes in all of Rhinestone. The Montgomery family had moved in eight years ago and Ruby still felt like the luckiest woman in the world, even though there were times where she missed the simplicity that their early years as a family had brought. When she and Jameson first got married, they had moved into a small one bedroom apartment in town and put Melanie's crib, once she joined their little family that next January, next to their bed. Ruby's mother took care of Melanie during the day while Ruby taught school and Jameson worked his way up the ladder at the law firm. Jameson bought some land near his grandparents and worked hard to clear the land every weekend that he wasn't at the office. Two years later they moved their toddler daughter into their sprawling home that they had all worked so hard on. Jameson quickly built a woodshop and made plans for a large barn to house his ultimate dream collection of antique tractors. He was still putting the finishing touches on his barn and had his eyes on a bass boat that the fishing store in Junction had just put on display. Ruby had a feeling that it wouldn't be long before they were eating fresh fish every weekend. Jameson loved to fish when he could find the time. As soon as Ruby told him the newly formed Ladies Auxiliary would be meeting one Saturday afternoon, he rounded up two of his buddies and made plans to spend the day on the river and in one of his friend's new 1971 red, white, and blue Rebel Fastback powered by a ninety-horsepower Mercury MerCruiser inboard-outboard engine. It was the finest model on the planet. Ruby didn't expect to see him 'til after dark. It wasn't often that Jameson got to spend all day on the river with his friends. He had worked very hard to become one of the top lawyers in the county. His dream was to one day own his own firm, just like his father.

While the group of ladies met in the living room, Maude kept Melanie company in the kitchen. The kitchen was Maude's favorite room of Magnolia Manor. There had already been so many wonderful dinners and desserts and holidays celebrated in that very room. The large bay window above the kitchen sink overlooked the grounds of the Manor that led to a line of trees in the forest where a gentle creek ran through the woods. Deer, rabbits, squirrels, chipmunks, opossums, shrews, foxes, and many species of birds roamed freely. The signature magnolia tree had grown considerably over the years. As far as they all knew, it was the only magnolia tree on the entire property. Jameson and Ruby owned fifty acres that mostly consisted of pastureland and a pine forest. It was heaven on earth as far as anyone was concerned. Opal had explored every square foot of the grounds over the years, but Maude was content to stay closer to the house.

Maude poured herself another glass of sweet tea and eyed the lemon cake that was almost done cooling on the counter. Ruby had promised her and Melanie a slice before she served it to the ladies in the living room.

Each lady had brought a covered dish or dessert. The pans and dishes covered the counter in the dining room which momentarily made Maude reconsider joining the group. As soon as the meeting was over, the plan was for them all to enjoy lunch together. Maude winked at Melanie, took a spoon from the drawer, and tested the potato salad that Lucille Adams had brought over. "Just as I expected, it's very good," Maude whispered. She smelled the pasta salad that Ellen Abernathy had brought but skipped over the covered pan that Nadine had brought just to be safe.

She could hear the ladies laughing from the next room over, but her attention was split between the smells of good southern cooking and the young girl who sighed heavily at the breakfast table. Melanie was bent over the table with a box of crayons and a stack of blank paper.

"What are you working on?" Maude asked.

"Mama said to be thinking about where to go on vacation this summer," Melanie frowned. "I think the beach sounds good, but my friend Janice at school said there's a new theme park opening in Florida like the one in California. Maybe I want to go there, too."

"I remember reading about that," Maude nodded. "But I don't think it'll be ready this summer. Why don't you make a list of things to do at the beach like you wanted first."

"Do you like to go to the beach?" Melanie asked.

"Sometimes," Maude nodded. "I think they need to invent a beach where there's not many people. I can't stand setting up my umbrella and someone I don't know walks over and tries to talk. I'm on vacation. They can leave me be."

Melanie giggled and went back to drawing her picture of a gigantic beach float in the middle of the ocean surrounded by dolphins. "I think Panama City would be a nice place to visit," Melanie suggested.

"There's even a theme park there," Maude said. She had liked the potato salad so much that she grabbed a bowl from the cabinet and served herself a large scoop. "Want some?"

"No thank you. Is there really a theme park in Panama City?" Melanie asked incredulously.

"Sure is. See if you can get your mama on one of those rides at the Miracle Strip," Maude chuckled. "It would be a miracle, I'll tell you what."

"What's Miracle Strip?" Melanie asked.

"Only the best amusement park in the world," Maude said knowingly, even though she had never been. "They have so many rides there. They even have this big old devil mouth you walk into and," but she was cut off by Ruby who gasped dramatically.

"Maude! What in the world are you talking about? A devil mouth? You should be ashamed!" Ruby frowned.

"What? At the Miracle Strip," Maude explained. "You know what I'm talking about!"

"How inappropriate," Nadine shook her head disapprovingly. She had followed Ruby into the kitchen to refill her water glass and wasn't at all surprised to hear such filth coming out of Maude's mouth. "And in front of a child!"

"Oh, can it, Nadine. I know for a fact you've been inside that mouth before!" Maude howled.

"Maude!" Ruby gasped. She was at a loss for words at how uncouth Maude was being.

"Well she has!" Maude continued. "She went on and on about it a few weeks ago. How come no one got their panties in a wad when she said it!"

"Maude!" Ruby repeated.

"Panties in a wad? I can assure you that they

aren't in a wad. I don't wear underwear, as a matter of fact," Nadine said.

"Can you both stop! Please!" Ruby interjected. She was sure that her face could not get any redder from sheer embarrassment. Melanie, on the other hand, was laughing hysterically at the two women arguing a few feet away from her.

"What's going on in here?" Opal asked as she waltzed into the kitchen. "And why are we discussing underwear?"

"We most certainly are not discussing that!" Ruby sighed. Opal merely shrugged and glanced over at the table at Melanie's drawing. "Is it arts and crafts time? Maude was never too good at that."

"It's the beach, aunt Opal," Melanie grinned.

"I love the beach," Opal exclaimed. "When are we going?"

"Maybe this summer," Melanie whispered hopefully. Opal winked at her and grabbed Ruby by the arm. "Come on, Rubes. Ellen's got a wild hair in there and thinks she may start a sock drive for the soldiers overseas. I need someone more sane than I am to talk her out of it."

"Socks? They don't need socks," Nadine grimaced. "They need far more than that. I told them to pause talking about things while I refilled my glass." She hurried out of the kitchen yelling as she ran.

"Oh goodness, we better get back in there!" Ruby frowned. "Maude, no more talking about whatever it was, please!"

Maude rolled her eyes and waited for Ruby and

Opal to return to their meeting. Once the coast was clear, she opened the nearest container and grabbed a few homemade chocolate chip cookies. She handed one to Melanie and together they ate the cookies and drank sweet tea while the ladies in the other room attempted to solve all the problems of the world.

"You know, one time I went with your mama and Opal to a beach twice the size of the one in Florida," Maude said. She finished her first cookie and started on the second.

Ruby and Jameson had eloped a few weeks after Ruby returned from her whirlwind of a trip across the world in 1960. She had, with Opal and Maude, spent a few weeks traveling to Italy by way of India, Nepal, and Albania, thanks to Opal's mistake in booking air travel. Naples and Nepal did have the same letters after all. Even though it was the wildest trip they had ever taken together, it held some of their favorite memories. It was also where Ruby discovered she was pregnant with Melanie. As soon as she got back to Rhinestone, she told Jameson and they decided to elope without any fanfare. They got married at the courthouse and spent a glorious weekend near Orange Beach before returning to Rhinestone as a married couple.

"It's high time she went back to the sand and water. And I better go along, too, just in case y'all get into any trouble," Maude continued.

"And aunt Opal, too?" Melanie asked.

"Of course! You can't have two of us without the other. It goes against nature," Maude said knowingly. "Though there was that time Opal went to a beach and pushed me off a cliff."

"When y'all went to Italy before I was born?" Melanie asked.

"That's right," Maude nodded. Opal had been dying to go cliff diving once they finally got to Positano, even though Maude was not too keen on the idea. For reasons she still didn't know herself, she ventured to the cliffs with Opal to see the beautiful view, only for Opal to suddenly push her off the cliff to the wide open sea below. It was an experience she would never forget, and one she hoped never to repeat. "That was a wild adventure, I tell you what! We crisscrossed the world and then back again. But I was much younger then."

"It wasn't that long ago," Melanie giggled.

"It feels like a lifetime ago," Maude replied. She brushed the crumbs off on her pants and drained the rest of her tea in her glass. "You know, it's been awhile since I've had a good vacation. We'll talk to your mama and daddy tonight and see what they think, but I think a summer beach trip sounds right as rain. As long as Opal doesn't plan it."

"Have you ever been to Panama City?" Melanie asked suddenly. She looked up from her drawing and studied Maude's face.

Maude found herself grinning, but she had to be careful how she answered the young girl's question. She has been to Panama City Beach many times, often during spring break and summer vacations with Ruby and Opal when they were in high school and during Ruby's college years. The three of them had soaked up a lot of rays on that stretch of sandy beach. Ruby had never joined in her and Opal's shenanigans, as she had always been the more mature one of the group. They all had some good times in the panhandle of Florida over the years. Some of those stories would never see the light of day.

They had never been to Miracle Strip, but Maude had to admit that her interests had been piqued after hearing Nadine ramble on about it after church one Sunday. She wasn't a thrill seeker by any means, but she loved to cut loose and have fun with the best of them. Plus, theme parks typically had delicious food that she couldn't find in Rhinestone, like funnel cakes, saltwater taffy, and footlong hot dogs. It was worth it to spend a few days at the beach for the food alone. The ocean oasis had the best seafood she had ever tasted. She couldn't say no to the all-you-could-eat crab buffets and fried fish baskets with hushpuppies and fries. She would never understand how Opal ate salad at the seafood shacks that were scattered along the beach.

Opal had been a vegetarian since she was a teenager. She knew it would be a lost cause to try and convince Maude to add more vegetables and fruits to her diet, so she took it upon herself to eat enough for the both of them. Maude would be perfectly content if she never ate any of what she called rabbit food. As far as she was concerned, people were put on earth to eat meat, and she ate more than her fair share most days. There wasn't a barbecue joint in the county that didn't know her by name.

"I think I hear them finishing up in there. I hope that means it's time to eat!" Maude said. The potato salad and chocolate chip cookies had not filled her up in the slightest.

The ladies filed into the kitchen and began filling their plates with potato salad, pasta salad, ham and cheese sliders, cookies, pimento cheese and crackers, and Ruby's rich lemon zest pound cake. It was a lunch fit for royalty.

"So, what did y'all come up with?" Maude asked.

"We discussed so many things!" Ruby exclaimed.

"So, you got nothing?" Maude asked. "It took y'all almost two hours to come up with that?"

"We had plenty of great ideas. This first meeting was just an introductory start anyway. Everything is going to work out perfectly," Nadine said. "It was my idea after all."

"Of course it was," Maude chuckled. "And the next meeting is when?"

"I wish I could tell you," Nadine said. "But unfortunately that's confidential. You have to be in the Auxiliary to know the details."

"There's still time to join, Maude," Opal grinned.

"I'm good," Maude replied.

Chapter Four

After a nice supper of fried catfish, hushpuppies, and coleslaw, the Montgomery family and their two closest friends ventured to the living room to relax. True to her word, Maude brought up the topic of summer vacation as she ate her two slices of iced lemon pound cake. It didn't take them all long to decide that a trip to the sunny seaside destination of Panama City Beach in Florida was the perfect choice for their summer vacation. Everyone seemed excited at the prospect of the waves and warm sand, though Maude made sure not to mention the devil's mouth ride again in front of Ruby.

"I'm glad you specified which Panama City you wanted to go to," Opal said.

"What do you mean?" Maude asked in between bites of cake.

Opal rolled her eyes at the lack of knowledge her friend was displaying. "There's more than one Panama City, Maude."

"Says who?" Maude questioned.

"She's right," Jameson chuckled. "But I highly doubt any of us want to venture over to Central America for a few days. Well, on second thought, maybe one day."

Maude did not look convinced. "Panama City Beach is in Florida. We've been there a million times."

"We've been to the one in Florida, yes," Opal nodded. "But not to the original one in Panama."

"I don't even know what you're talking about," Maude yawned.

"She never did pay attention in school," Opal whispered to Melanie who was watching the two women go back and forth. "This is a prime example of why you should pay attention to your teacher and focus on your studies."

As the evening wore on, the conversation took a more somber turn as the evening news came on the television. Melanie was sent upstairs to take a bath and get ready for bed while the four adults watched the nightly news full of black and white images of a land far away.

"Anyone we know?" Maude asked bluntly.

Jameson shook his head. "No one that I've heard lately. I know another unit from over yonder got home last week. I haven't been to a service since Joseph Williams' last month. That one was hard."

"I thought it was supposed to be over," Maude sighed. The leaders in Washington had made so many decisions over the years that hadn't made much sense to the average person. Thousands of troops had been withdrawn and redeployed and withdrawn again. It seemed to be never ending.

"Who could say," Ruby frowned. "I just don't understand it."

"They're asking too much of these kids," Maude sighed.

"Some aren't kids," Opal nodded. "And some really are children. I can't even read the newspaper anymore."

"I remember when my uncle Woodrow came back in 1944. Well, not when he came back, but for years afterwards he would just disappear. He'd be gone for a week at a time," Ruby frowned.

"He used to sit under the porch of the house," Maude nodded. "I remember that."

Ruby nodded. Her uncle Woodrow had been at Normandy and never spoke of his time in the military or overseas. The only time it was ever brought up was when he would have one of his episodes, as they were referred to, and he'd lock all the doors of his house and hide in his bedroom with his gun or when he'd be found asleep underneath the front porch with his canteen. He had passed away fifteen years ago from liver failure. The only solace he ever found was at the bottom of a whiskey bottle.

"I got a letter from Thomas this morning," Opal said suddenly. She pulled it out of her purse and held onto it gingerly. "Of course it doesn't say anything that we didn't already know, but at least he sounds like he's doing ok."

She passed the piece of paper around to the others in the room to let them read it. Once she had it back, she carefully folded it and placed it back in her purse. She kept every handwritten letter she had ever received in a trunk in her bedroom, along with every other special memento that meant something dear to her.

Her cousin Thomas was a medic in the United States Army. Opal was sure that he had seen the absolute worst of humanity during his time in the warzone, but his letters never mentioned anything tragic. She knew that he was probably trying to be brave for her sake, but she knew the peril that he was in daily. She also knew that he wasn't able to write everything in a letter in case it was intercepted. He was supposed to be protected. It was a known war crime to fire on a medic, but protections didn't matter out there in the heat of war. He had a very dangerous job and he worried her just as much, if not more, than all of the other people she wrote letters to.

She remembered playing with Thomas when they were kids at family reunions. He was only two years her junior, but it felt like just yesterday they were trying to see who could run the fastest and the farthest. Now Thomas was in the military and no matter how fast or far he ran, he was surrounded by war.

He had been drafted in 1969 at the age of twenty-eight. Most of U.S. soldiers drafted during the Vietnam War were men from poor and working-class families. These were young men who were not going get a college deferment, have a political connection, or have a family doctor that could give them a medical deferment. Not that Thomas would have chosen to use any of those routes anyway. He was proud to represent his country, but it had been obvious for Opal to discern a change in his letters as time wore on.

Thomas was always exhausted. There was always something going on, even when the guns weren't firing around him. Medics and corpsmen on the battlefields of Vietnam were focused mainly on treatment and evacuation for wounded troops. They had to always be ready for whatever was to come. They stopped the bleeding, managed pain the best they knew how to, and did whatever else was necessary to keep troops alive until they could be evacuated elsewhere. It was men like Thomas who tried to keep death at bay during the most crucial periods. They often fought alongside their friends. Opal knew that Thomas carried a rifle along with his medical kit. Even when they weren't under fire, medics were essential to the health and wellness of their units. According to different programs on the television, men like Thomas also treated South Vietnamese villagers, overlooking the possibility that some of them might be enemy combatants or sympathizers. That would be something Thomas would do. He had a heart of gold and would never overlook a person, regardless of their appearance.

The good news was that Thomas would be coming home sometime later this year. He had written Opal all about his plans. Once he was out of the military, he planned on working with his father at the hospital until he could afford a few acres of land on his own. After seeing and experiencing everything that he had in the military, he wanted nothing more than open land and vast skies. He craved peace above all else. Opal thought that every person deserved that, especially American heroes.

"I'm going to leave you three to do what it is y'all do," Jameson said after a while. "I've got a big meeting in the morning that I'm hoping finally gets the ball rolling on that case over in Birmingham." He kissed Ruby on the top of her head and walked down the hallway to his office.

"Birmingham, huh?" Opal asked once the office door closed.

Ruby nodded. "He's been in the Birmingham office most days for the last two weeks. Some construction company trying to settle something with one of their workers."

"It's always something," Maude agreed. She yawned loudly and stretched her arms over the head. "Can we turn the channel to something else?"

"What would you like to watch?" Ruby asked. She stretched as she stood up from her recliner and walked over to the television that had long been tuned out. She checked the clock on the wall and then looked back at the television. "I don't know what all would be on right now."

"Who needs the television!" Opal chirped. "Let's do the crossword instead."

"That's boring," Maude frowned.

"It's anything but!" Opal gasped. "Normally I do the crossword alone, but I'm willing to spread the knowledge around every now and again."

"That sounds fun," Ruby said. She sank back into the recliner and waited for Opal to begin.

"Alright, let's see," Opal bit the end of her pen and scanned the newspaper for the best clue to share. "Ok, three down is a tough one." She looked at Maude and frowned slightly. "I don't think you'll know this one, but Ruby might." Before Maude could retort, Opal cleared her throat and read the clue. "A spoon-shaped vessel with a long handle. Five letters."

"Scoop," Maude yelled confidently.

Opal shook her head. "No, I don't think that's it."

"It's five letters," Maude shrugged.

"Try ladle," Ruby suggested.

"Exactly," Opal nodded.

"Scoop is five letters," Maude countered.

"I don't think I've ever heard a ladle referred to as a scoop," Ruby chuckled.

"Scoop is a much better name than ladle," Maude replied.

"Why don't you make that your next project," Opal giggled. "Since you aren't so keen on joining the Auxiliary and all."

"I've got better things to do than gossip and save the world with you old biddies," Maude teased.

Opal gasped in mock surprise. "I'm still a spring chicken, thank you very much!"

Ruby rolled her eyes and asked Opal to read the next clue.

"The capital of Peru, four letters," Opal read.

"The capital of Peru? How the hell should I know?" Maude scoffed.

"Four letters," Opal said again.

"Not helping," Maude retorted.

"I think I know," Ruby said. "Lime?"

"Close!" Opal squealed. "Lima."

"Lima? Geez, Opal, if you knew the answer, why'd you even ask us?" Maude asked.

"You're the one who wanted to play the crossword," Opal shrugged. "I can't help that I already know all the answers."

"For someone so dadgum crazy, you're pretty smart," Maude uttered.

"That may be the nicest thing you've ever said to me," Opal chuckled.

"Oh goodness, while you two argue I'm going to go tuck Melly into bed. I swear, you two are making me gray!" Ruby laughed. Maude and Opal continued to bicker playfully while Ruby went upstairs. When she came down a few minutes later, she asked her two friends if they had made any progress.

"Not really," Opal shrugged. "Maude's too busy going on and on about Max."

"Max Willford?" Ruby asked. "I didn't get the impression that you were too keen on him."

"I'm not," Maude agreed. "He's worse than the lint between my toes."

"Why do you have lint between your toes?" Opal asked. "You really need to get a handle on that. At your age you shouldn't be having these kind of issues."

"Oh shut up," Maude sighed. "I'm just saying he's annoying."

"Then why do you keep seeing him?" Opal asked.

"Not all of us have a beau of the week," Maude replied.

"You should never settle," Opal admonished.

"I know, it's just that sometimes it's nice to have someone to go to dinner with," Maude shrugged.

"What are we, chopped liver?" Opal gasped playfully.

"You know what I mean," Maude smiled. "Anyway, I think it's about time I stopped returning his phone calls. There's only so much smell I can take."

"Oh, not that again," Opal gagged. "He can't help that he works with animals all day."

"But he can help washing his," Maude squealed, but Ruby quickly cut her off before she could finish. "Well, I'm just saying." Max Willford was one of the most in demand veterinarians in the tri-county area. His knowledge and affable spirit with animals and their owners was second to none. The only thing that matched his talents and intelligence was the fact that he often smelled like manure. He wasn't keen on making time to shower off or change his clothes before picking Maude up for dinner after he closed his vet practice in the evenings.

"Eight across," Opal interjected. "Romeo's tragic love interest."

"Julie," Maude nodded confidently. "No wait, Juliet."

"That's right!" Opal exclaimed.

"Always the tone of surprise," Maude shrugged. "Read us another one."

"What city does the NFL team Cowboys play in?" Opal asked.

"I know!" Jameson called out from his office.

"All together now," Maude laughed. "Dallas!"

"Dallas is an amazing place to visit," Opal said as she penciled in the correct letters. "I'll never forget my time there a few years ago."

"Best steak I ever had," Maude nodded.

"I meant the history and the people," Opal explained.

"That's because you don't eat beef," Maude said. "You don't know what you're missing."

"I can't believe y'all got to see where the President was killed," Ruby said quietly. "I bet it was a chilling experience for sure."

"It sure was," Maude nodded. All three women shuddered at the memories of the assassination of John Fitzgerald Kennedy from a few years before. It had been unlike anything any of them had experienced before. They each remembered exactly where they were the moment they heard about the tragedy.

"Well on that note, I better be getting home," Opal said. "I've got a big day tomorrow. A big week really."

"That's right!" Ruby exclaimed. "You're going to Charleston this week for the conference."

"Yes ma'am," Opal smiled. "I've got to pack still, but that shouldn't take too long."

"Why do you always wait to the last minute to pack?" Ruby giggled.

"Because I never know what I'll need," Opal shrugged. "Anyway, Ms. Belva and I are leaving around ten in the morning. We'll be back Friday, so please keep an eye on my house and Leo. Don't forget about him, Maude. You know how he gets."

"That damn cat, I swear," Maude sassed.

"You promised," Opal reminded her.

"I'll keep an eye on him," Maude nodded. "But I'm not feeding him."

"Maude!" Ruby gasped. "He's a precious animal. You have to feed him or he'll starve."

"I don't mean it like that! I mean I ain't gonna set him up at the kitchen table and feed him with a spoon," Maude retorted. "That is beyond insane."

"It's what he prefers," Opal shrugged. She grabbed her purse and waited for Maude to put her jacket on. Once Maude was ready, the three women took their plates and cups to the kitchen and set them in the sink.

"Have a great trip, Opal," Ruby smiled. "I can't wait to hear all about it once you get home."

"I can't wait to bring back all the new and upcoming products from the big city," Opal grinned. "It's going to be amazing."

Chapter Five

For the first time in her life, Opal was packed and ready for a trip early. It always aggravated Maude and Ruby that Opal was so lackadaisical with her time when it came to trips and vacations. However, this was no ordinary trip. This was a trip to Charleston to one of the biggest hair care conferences Opal had ever been to. Mrs. Belva was set to pick her up around ten, and Opal knew better than to be a minute later. Belva Sinclair waited for no one. There was a rumor that she had left her second husband at the altar after he was five minutes late to their wedding.

At ten o'clock on the dot, Belva Sinclair's 1970 cherry red Ford Mustang came into view. She honked the horn as Opal bustled outside with her purse and gigantic suitcase. She tossed the suitcase in the back seat and met Belva's smile with one of her own. "Are you ready for the show of a lifetime?" Belva grinned. She was already backing out of the driveway before Opal could adjust her hair in the side mirror.

"Absolutely!" Opal yelled.

Belva spun her tires and flew down the highway towards Atlanta, the first stop on their trip. Belva knew all the ins and outs of the south. There wasn't a food or drink joint that Belva Sinclair hadn't been to and thoroughly enjoyed in her fifty-five years on earth. Opal idolized her, and the feeling was mutual. Belva had never taken on an apprentice in her career until Opal Tyler came along. It was no secret that one day all of Belva's fortune would be passed onto the brilliant woman in her passenger seat. Not that Belva was planning on retiring anytime soon, but it was nice to have a protegee on hand for when that time came.

Meanwhile back in Rhinestone, Maude was on the floor of the greasy garage underneath a 1962 Ducati Scrambler. It was the third time in the past year that her neighbor, Willie Hamilton, had brought it in for something or another. Willie was a good kid, but he didn't have any business riding a motorcycle. Everyone in town knew they better stay out of his way on account of his not knowing how to operate it. This time he had laid it down over the railroad tracks near Hopper Street right past the train depot. Maude cursed under her breath as she untangled what could only be splinters from railroad ties from the front wheel. Willie was lucky that the danged train hadn't drug him down the tracks.

Two hours later, Willie sheepishly thanked her for fixing his most prized possession once again. "You're the best, Ms. Cooper. See you next time!" Maude swore that if she saw him wheeling it in again, she'd close the garage door in his face.

Maude knew more about cars and motorcycles than most men in Rhinestone combined. The faster the car or motorcycle, the more she loved it. It was love at first sight when she saw the sleek black body of the Pontiac GTO sitting on the nearby car lot. She didn't even think twice before she drove it off the lot towards the wide open highway that led to Junction. She didn't mind the two speeding tickets she talked her way out of within a month's time either. Those were expected when you drove such a beast of a car.

Ruby nor Opal would ever ride with her. She wasn't sure why. Neither of them had ever died or been remotely injured when they were in her car. They often took Ruby's more practical car when they traveled together, but one of the days Maude was going to put the hammer down and take those two on a joyride of their lives.

"Come on, Ruby! Just one lap around the block," Maude pleaded with Ruby over lunch.

"The fact that you call it a lap like it's some NASCAR race," Ruby frowned.

"I'll put the windows down and let the wind blow through your hair!" Maude continued.

Ruby shot her a look that would have withered most of her students, but it didn't faze Maude. She was more than used to Ruby's looks of concern and annoyance.

"You need to live a little! You'll change your mind one of these days," Maude shrugged. She drank the rest of her sweet tea and looked longingly at the last slice of almond pound cake on the counter.

"Go on and eat it," Ruby laughed. "Jameson took a piece for lunch already and Melanie informed me that almond cake is no longer her favorite."

"Her loss," Maude said. She practically inhaled the moist cake and then licked the icing off her fingers.

Ruby ignored her friend's antics and stared out the window. "I'm glad we didn't go anywhere for spring break this year. I'm too tired to go anyway."

"I hear that," Maude nodded. "I wonder what Opal's up to? They should be close to Charleston by now."

"Depends on how many times they stopped along the way," Ruby said. "Knowing those two, they could be in Tennessee for all we know."

"They sure do have a good time together," Maude nodded. "I wouldn't want to hang out with my boss, but then again, it's my dad and uncle, so maybe I would." She and Ruby laughed away the afternoon before Maude had to get back to the garage and Ruby retired to the kitchen table to grade some papers.

Ruby loved teaching the children of Rhinestone. Many of them were hungry to learn and it didn't hurt that everyone knew everyone in town. She didn't often have to threaten to call someone's mama more than once.

"Mama, I'm bored," Melanie said as she walked downstairs around four o'clock that afternoon. She had been looking forward to her sabbatical from school on her spring break vacation, but she was already bored out of her mind. She had already read every book she had checked out from the library and played with all her toys. Her best friend had gone to the beach with her family, so she was even more bored than usual.

"Have you done all your chores?" Ruby asked without looking up from the lined paper in front of her.

"Yes ma'am. I took out the trash and cleaned up my room. I even wiped down the counter in the bathroom," she frowned. She looked out the window and saw the dark clouds that had been in the sky all afternoon. "When's this storm gonna blow over?"

"Not 'til tomorrow," Ruby answered. "Would you like to help me get started on supper in a few minutes? We have plenty of time to make some peanut butter cookies if you like."

"Yes ma'am," Melanie grinned. Even though she wasn't too keen on the meatloaf that Jameson had requested for tonight, she loved peanut butter cookies. "Can we do some more of that puzzle tonight, too?"

"Of course! You know your daddy would love that," Ruby smiled. Jameson had been away at a work conference for the past few days in Nashville and both Ruby and Melanie were ready to see him.

When Jameson got home a few hours later, he walked in the front door to the smells of fresh peanut butter cookies on the counter and a pan of meatloaf in the oven. "Smells good!" Jameson grinned. He kissed Ruby and then hugged Melanie who was too busy eating peanut butter out of the jar to notice her father enter in the archway behind her. "Want some?" she asked him with her mouth full.

"No thanks," he laughed. "Let me go set this stuff down and I'll come help make the tea."

"Supper will be ready in thirty minutes," Ruby called out from the pantry.

As the sun began to set Thursday evening, casting its warm golden hues through the kitchen window, Jameson walked back inside from his home office door to the aroma of freshly baked bread filling the tidy kitchen. It had been a long few days for Jameson as he had been a few hours away at the conference in Nashville, Tennessee. Ruby hurried to get supper on the table while Melanie sat at the kitchen table, her notebook open, working on some school assignments. As she noticed her dad clearing his throat, she looked up with a smile.

"Hey, sweetie," Jameson said, dropping his keys on the table and walking over to Melanie. "How's the homework going?"

"It's going okay," she answered, looking up at him. "I think I'm finally getting the hang of it."

"Good for you!" Jameson beamed, leaning down to give her a quick hug. "I'm proud of you."

Ruby glanced over her shoulder from the stove, her eyes softening. Jameson smiled and kissed his wife on the cheek before settling into the chair at the table. "It's so good to be home."

Melanie, who had been scribbling in her notebook, looked up with curiosity and scrunched her nose. "How was work? It sounds boring."

"Boring? Not at all," Jameson chuckled. "There were some really interesting sessions, actually. It was about new legal practices and ethics in law. Lawyers from all over the country gathered to discuss changes in the legal landscape, new challenges in the courtroom, and innovations in technology. But you know what? I'm not sure you'd want to hear all about that part of it," he said, with a playful wink.

Melanie giggled. "Probably not, unless you're going to make me a lawyer like you!"

"Maybe someday, if that's what you want," he said, his voice softening. "But for now, let's just say it was a lot of talking, a lot of presentations, and lots of coffee." Jameson paused, a thoughtful look on his face. "But what I really enjoyed was the city itself, Nashville, I mean. It was a beautiful place. So much history, culture, and of course, great music everywhere you go. We'll have to go one day."

"I like country music," Melanie said intently.

"Me, too," Jameson said, sitting back in his chair and folding his arms. "You know Nashville is known as the Music City, right? The whole town feels like a big stage, with live bands playing in every restaurant and on the street corners."

"Whoa, that sounds fun!" Melanie's eyes lit up. "Was it like what we see on television?"

"Pretty much," Jameson nodded. "Though a lot of it was more about the history behind the music. It was fascinating. Nashville's music scene is such a big part of the city's identity. People go there to see legendary musicians perform, but also to experience the culture."

Ruby, who had been listening intently, turned around from the stove. "Sounds like you had a good time."

"Well," Jameson began, "there's a lot of great food in Nashville, too. I had some of the best barbecue I've ever tasted, and the hot chicken? Spicy, but delicious!"

Melanie wrinkled her nose. "Hot chicken? What's that?"

Jameson laughed. "It's a fried chicken dish with a special hot sauce that makes your mouth burn but also makes you want more. It's a Nashville staple. You'd probably need a tall glass of sweet tea to cool it down, though!"

"I think I'll pass on that," Melanie said, sticking out her tongue.

The Montgomery family had a nice meal of meatloaf, peas, and rice together at the dining room table. Melanie managed to eat enough of her meatloaf so Ruby allowed her two cookies for an evening snack. While Melanie devoured her cookies, Jameson snuck into his office and returned with a white bag that clearly had something in it. "I thought you might like something from Tennessee."

Melanie carefully opened the bag to reveal a new jigsaw puzzle. The front of the box showed a giant acoustic guitar with different colored cowboy boots and hats around the edges. It had one thousand pieces. Jameson had admitted to Ruby that he was too focused on the picture on the front of the box and didn't notice the piece count.

"A puzzle!" Melanie exclaimed. "This is great! Thank you!"

"You're welcome, sweetheart," Jameson

replied. "I thought you might enjoy putting it together. It'll be like having a little piece of Nashville here with us."

Ruby came over to the table and gave Melanie a quick kiss on the cheek. "It's a great souvenir. I'm sure you'll have fun with it."

Melanie looked up at her dad, holding the puzzle close to her chest. "I can't wait to start it! Will you help me?"

"Of course I will. I'm glad you like it," Jameson said, then looked over at Ruby. "I didn't forget about you either." From his bag, he pulled out a cookbook, the cover decorated with images of southern dishes like fried green tomatoes, cornbread, and a pie that looked so rich it could have come straight from heaven. "It's a Nashville cookbook, full of country cooking recipes. I thought you might enjoy trying some new recipes for dinner. It has everything from appetizers to desserts, all the southern comforts you love."

Ruby's eyes lit up as she took the cookbook from him. "This is perfect! I've been wanting to try some new recipes. Maybe I'll make us some of that hot chicken you were talking about."

"Be careful with the heat level," Jameson teased. "But if you do, make sure we have plenty of sweet tea on hand."

Ruby chuckled. "I'll start with something a little less spicy, but I'm excited to dive into this. Thanks, honey. This is a thoughtful gift. Why don't you two go on into the living room and get started on that puzzle. I'll be in directly once I get the dishes washed."

"I've got you one more thing here," Jameson smiled. He pulled a velvet jewelry box out of his pocket and handed it to Ruby. Ruby opened it gingerly and saw a beautiful locket with Melanie's initials engraved on it. "This is beautiful," she smiled.

"I passed by this little jewelry shop every morning and couldn't not go inside," he grinned.

"I love it. Thank you," Ruby said. Jameson helped her put it on and smiled. "It looks perfect. He then poured himself a glass of milk and grabbed a few cookies and met his daughter in the living room to work on their puzzle that was spread all over the coffee table. Ruby did the dishes and then joined her husband and daughter in the living room as they tried to figure out which piece went where. She didn't want to break their concentration, so she decided to finish grading the papers she hadn't quite finished. After twenty minutes of mental work, Melanie threw her hands up in the air and said, "I give up! This is too hard."

"You should ask Opal to help once she's back home from her conference," Ruby offered.

"Great idea," Jameson nodded. "I've never seen a puzzle that Opal can't do."

"Really?" Melanie giggled. "I've never seenher sit still enough for a puzzle."

"That's true, too," Jameson nodded. "Her mind works in special ways though."

"Let me see about this puzzle," Ruby said. She set the stack of papers and her red pen on the end table and joined Melanie and Jameson on the floor. After another fifteen minutes, Jameson smiled at Melanie over Ruby's head. They were finally making noticeable progress.

Chapter Six

Opal and Belva had the time of their lives in Charleston. In fact, the city of Charleston may never be the same after those two swept through it. By the time they made their way back to Rhinestone, not only was Miss Belva's car loaded down with the finest hair care products this side of the Mississippi, but it was also filled to the gills with the latest fashions of the east coast elite. Opal had the grand idea of turning part of the salon into a boutique for the women of Rhinestone, and she nor Belva wanted to come back to town empty-handed. They had samples of the finest clothes and shoes that would be sure to entice the fancy ladies of Rhinestone's upper crust.

Pastels were in and Belva had wasted little time in filling the backseat of her car with flare-legged pants with a drop waist, large belts, and matching shirts with outrageous prints. There were quite a few classier outfits draped over the seat that could have been designed by Jackie O. herself. After she dropped Opal off at her house, Belva rushed to the salon and began unloading her many treasures. She would have to spend all night leaving these gorgeous finds as she knew they wouldn't stay in the window for long.

Opal didn't waste any time getting Ruby and Maude back in her salon chair once she was unpacked from her trip. While Melanie attended her next Girl Scouts of America meeting after school on Friday, Ruby let Opal try out some of her new hair care products on her. Maude never liked a fuss and generally refused to let Opal do anything with her hair other than trim it every few weeks, but even she couldn't turn down the sleek oil that kept the tiny flyaways from poking her in the eye. Opal gasped when Maude smiled at herself in the mirror and perfected the look by putting her ratty baseball cap back on.

"You ruined it!" Opal cried.

"How so?" Maude retorted.

"Why do you always have to wear that disgusting old hat?" Opal pouted.

"It's not disgusting!" Maude sassed. "It's just well worn."

"It has dirt and God knows what else all over it. It's probably home to some new kind of mold and space creatures," Opal pointed out.

"It wouldn't hurt to clean it now and then," Ruby added.

Maude turned to Ruby and shook her head vigorously. "Cleaning it would ruin it! This is my lucky hat. I've never once washed it a day in my life. If I washed it, the team would lose for sure."

"I've never understood your silly little superstitions," Ruby scoffed and rolled her eyes.

"This hat ain't a superstition, it's a fact. Every time I wear this to a game we win. That one time I left it at home we lost!" Maude sighed.

Opal and Ruby both rolled their eyes again. Maude wasn't the best at keeping track of her beloved baseball team that had a losing record worse than the Chicago Bears. "I'm just saying that a little rinse might not hurt it," Ruby suggested. "Or a good boil on the stove."

Maude shook her head again and Ruby and Opal gave up arguing with her. After a few minutes of relative silence, Maude yawned loudly. "I'm bored," she pouted.

"Then grab that broom over yonder and sweep up that pile of hair by the counter," Opal directed. She smoothed a thick white paste through Ruby's long hair and combed it through.

"Not that kind of bored," Maude pouted. "I'm bored here in Rhinestone. You know every now and then I get the itch to go somewhere."

"You know they make creams for that," said Opal as she giggled.

Maude turned a vivid shade of pink which made Opal giggle even harder. "Y'all to be quiet. You can't talk about stuff like that. It's private," Ruby whispered.

"I didn't say where she had to put it," Opal shrugged.

This time Ruby matched Maude's shade of pink. Opal knew how to turn a conversation inappropriate in a matter of seconds. It was part of her charm. There was no telling what she could come up with at the drop of a hat.

"Opal Tyler, I swear," Ruby muttered.

"You shouldn't swear," Opal grinned. "That's

never been your thing. Leave the swearing to Maude."

"I don't cuss as much as I used to," Maude shrugged.

"Aw, our little devil is growing up," Opal chuckled.

Maude stuck her tongue out at Opal and sighed loudly. "I'm hungry."

"You're always hungry," Opal shrugged.

"I thought you were bored?" Ruby asked.

"Bored and hungry, same thing," Maude said.

"Why don't you go pick us up something from Harriet's?" Opal suggested.

"Ooh," Ruby perked up. "If she has lemon pie, get me a slice, please."

"I can't go back to Harriet's," Maude frowned.

"Why not?" Ruby asked.

"You got kicked out of another business," Opal suggested.

"Another business?" Ruby asked. "What is she talking about, Maude?"

"Yes, Maude, what could I possibly be referring to?" Opal giggled.

"Nothing," Maude said too quickly.

"What's going on?" Ruby asked. "You didn't get kicked out of a business did you?"

"It ain't exactly a business," Maude said quietly.

Opal shook her head. "Maude got kicked out of the library over in Junction yesterday morning."

"Maude!" Ruby gasped. "A library! Really? What did you do? That's almost as bad as getting kicked out of church!"

"Well, honestly I figured you'd be just as

surprised as I was that Maude knew what a library was in the first place," Opal began.

"Oh can it," Maude interrupted. "I was just trying to return my library books."

"Maude, you know darn well you weren't returning library books," Opal cackled. "We both know you don't read."

"I know how to read!" Maude exclaimed.

"I didn't say you couldn't, I said you choose not to," Opal corrected.

"Do I even want to know?" Ruby asked.

"She rode over to the library with me so I could donate some of Ms. Belva's older magazines. I left Maude in the car, but when I came out I caught her! She was snooping to see what books Nadine had just dropped in that little book return box," Opal laughed.

"Maude!" Ruby all but shouted.

"I was just trying to see what she was reading. Just making sure it wasn't anything inappropriate," Maude shrugged.

Ruby shook her head and rolled her eyes. "I still don't see why you got kicked out of the library though."

"I'll explain," Opal grinned. "You see, Maude was trying to fit her arm through the slit where the books fit and she got stuck."

"What?" Ruby's eyes widened.

"Literally stuck," Opal sighed. "I was embarrassed. Well, I would have been embarrassed if I actually got embarrassed, but that's neither here nor there, I suppose."

"You ain't never been embarrassed in your

life," Maude sassed.

"Can y'all stay on topic for once," Ruby pleaded.

"Ruby! They had to call the fire department to cut the box in half to get her arm out," Opal laughed.

"It's not funny," Maude scowled. "I've still got bruises on my arm."

"I cannot believe you, Maude! Well, I can, but Lord!" Ruby said.

"I'm surprised you didn't hear about it," Opal said. "It was all anyone's been talking about since."

"Ruby doesn't listen to gossip," Maude huffed.

"I don't think that's gossip," Opal replied. "I saw it happen with my own three eyes."

"Three eyes?" Ruby asked.

"Don't get her started," Maude interjected. "Opal with the eyes in the back of her head or whatever mumbo jumbo she goes on and on about."

"You two are always getting off topic. Why can't you go over to Harriet's and get some pie?" Opal asked.

"Because that man has ruined Harriet's for me," Maude frowned. "He couldn't find his own ass with two hands."

"What man?" Ruby asked.

"Is there a man in your life?" Opal asked.

"No!" Maude huffed.

"That rude man from lunch the other day?" Ruby asked.

"Yes," Maude said. ""That creatin from Sunday. I should've knocked him into the middle of next week!"

"Next time you can. Now can you get us some pie," Opal smiled.

"Fine," Maude said. "But if I see him, I'm shoving him into the library box." She grabbed her purse and stomped out the front door to her motorcycle.

"You don't think she'd really hurt that man, do you?" Ruby asked Opal.

"Of course I do," Opal nodded. "He'd deserve it, too."

Opal swept the floor and tidied up her station while Ruby read a magazine in the chair. "Opal, have you heard anything from Thomas this week?"

"I sent him a care package this morning," Opal said.

"That's nice," Ruby smiled.

"Ruby, can I tell you something?" Opal asked quickly.

Ruby set down the magazine and turned to face Opal. "What's wrong?"

"I don't know," Opal sighed. "I just have this terrible feeling in my gut. I can't explain it, Rubes."

"A terrible feeling about Maude or what do you mean?" Ruby asked carefully.

"No, not Maude. There's no helping her," Opal smiled. "I don't know really. I just have this ominous feeling that something is wrong."

"Oh Opal, I'm so sorry to hear that. What can I do?" Ruby asked sincerely.

Opal smiled and patted Ruby on the shoulder. "Oh, it's probably just me being silly. I'm sure everything is fine. I'm just exhausted from the conference and Maude's antics."

"Are you still going on about that?" Maude huffed. She set two brown paper bags on the counter and began to rifle through them. "They didn't have lemon, but there was a chocolate cream pie and a key lime. I didn't know which one y'all wanted, so I got both."

"We can't eat two whole pies," Ruby gasped.

"Speak for yourself, Ruby," Maude said. She pulled a metal fork from her purse and wiped it off on her shirt. "Yes, I keep a fork handy at all times for situations like this."

"I wasn't even going to ask," Ruby said.

"Chocolate or key lime?" Maude asked.

"Key lime," Ruby and Opal said at the same time. Maude handed out the slices of pie on napkins and then dug into the chocolate pie on her own.

"No thanks, we didn't want any chocolate," Opal giggled as Maude demolished the piped whipped cream on top of the chocolate pie. Chocolate shavings fell to the floor as Maude shrugged. "I'm a growing girl," she burped.

"Classy," Opal laughed. They finished their pie in relative silence except for an occasional sound of the scraping fork against the pie tin.

"That was good," Maude said.

"It was," Ruby nodded. She looked up at the clock on the wall and noted the time. "It's almost time to pick up Melanie. I hope she had a great time! This could be so good for her." She shook her hair loose and threw away her napkin in the trash can full of hair products and hair clippings.

"I'll ride over with you if you want," Maude

offered.

"Sure!" Ruby said. "Want to tag along, Opal?"

"I wish I could," Opal said. "I'm going to finish up here and then take aunt Willie to her appointment."

"What appointment?" Maude said.

"I don't really know," Opal shrugged. "She said she has some appointment down the river. We're taking her canoe and should be back later tonight."

"Forget I asked," Maude said. "The less I know about your aunt Wilhemina's antics the better."

"Sounds like an adventure," Ruby smiled. "Alright, Opal, we'll see you at church on Sunday if not before."

"Can't wait to hear about Melly's new adventure," Opal said. "If she needs any help with any projects, let me know."

"Of course," Ruby nodded. She hugged Opal and whispered, "I'll call you tomorrow."

Once Ruby and Maude were in Ruby's car, Maude sighed and said, "I'm worried about Opal."

"Why?" Ruby asked. She backed out of the parking space and drove towards the highway.

"After I got my arm loose, I heard her talking to one of those library ladies about a book program or something. She looked real sad when the lady said that most of the books don't get returned," Maude explained.

"Oh," Ruby said. "She must have been talking about the book exchange program she started with the men overseas. Oh, Maude, they don't get returned because, well, I don't want to say it."

"Yea," Maude nodded pensively. "That's what

I was afraid of. This is getting to be too much for her. She's got to stop getting so involved. She already writes a dozen or so letters a week. And you know she won't miss an event at the VA. She's running herself ragged. She's gotta slow down."

"That will never happen," Ruby said. "Opal's got a heart two miles wide. We've just got to make sure we're helping her as best we can."

"I guess I could maybe write some letters for her pen pal program," Maude conceded. "And yes, I remember how to write."

"I know you do," Ruby chuckled. "I just hope they can read your unique scrawl."

"You sound like all my old teachers from school," Maude teased. "My handwriting ain't that bad."

Melanie climbed in the backseat as soon as Ruby pulled into the parking spot in front of the school. Melanie looked happy which made Ruby feel good. She had been so worried about her daughter not being able to find a hobby that suited her. Piano lessons hadn't lasted longer than three weeks and Melanie said she wouldn't be caught dead in a cheerleading uniform.

"Oh mama! It was so fun! We made picture frames and ate trail mix. They told us all about the different badges we can earn!" Melanie exclaimed.

"That's wonderful!" Ruby smiled. "I can't wait to hear all about it."

"What's for supper?" Melanie asked.

"Yea, what's for supper?" Maude asked.

"You're hungry already?" Ruby asked. "You just ate an entire pie not an hour ago."

"That was then, this is now," Maude shrugged.

"Jameson has to work late tonight, so I was thinking we could pick up a pizza if that sounds good," Ruby offered.

"Yes!" Melanie squealed.

"Want to join us, Maude?" Ruby asked.

"As long as it's not one of those weird pizzas like Opal orders. No one likes spinach and olives on their pizza. Or the pineapple one she got last week. Just plain old pineapples. Pizza was made for pepperonis and ham and sausage," Maude said.

"Pepperoni it is," Ruby laughed.

"Drop me off at my bike and I'll run by my house and get the lemon loaf I picked up yesterday from the Pig. You got any ice cream at your house or should I bring my own?" Maude asked.

"I think there's some in the freezer," Ruby said. "If Jameson hasn't gotten into it yet. You know he has to eat his small bowl of vanilla ice cream every night before bed."

"I'll bring some just in case," Maude said. "I'll be over to the Manor directly."

Ruby pulled up next to Maude's motorcycle and noticed that Opal's car was already gone. The closed sign had been hung on the door of the salon and the parking lot was nearly empty. Ruby let Maude peel out of the parking lot before she slowly backed out of the spot. She and Melanie drove to the local pizza parlor that was quite busy for a Friday evening. They waited patiently for their pizza and once it was brought to the counter, Ruby handed it to Melanie to carry to the car. As soon as they entered the driveway, Ruby saw that

Maude was waiting for them on the front porch with a shopping bag full of ice cream cartons and a wrapped lemon loaf under her arm.

"Did you have to bring the entire freezer aisle?" Ruby asked.

"I couldn't decide which flavor I'd want later, so I brought a few different options," Maude shrugged.

They spent the evening eating pizza and ice cream with the television turned off. A cozy evening at Magnolia Manor needed not be interrupted by the chaos going on in the world.

Chapter Seven

"Let's build a birdhouse," Jameson suggested Sunday afternoon. The early spring sun was only slightly obscured by the thin white clouds that resembled paint brush strokes across the blue sky.

"I don't really want to build one," Melanie pouted. She closed the book she had been reading and frowned up at her father.

"Why not?" Jameson asked gently.

"Birds are scary," Melanie shrugged.

"Scary?" Jameson repeated. "Why are they scary?"

"I don't know," Melanie pouted. "They're loud and squawk all the time. One time that bird chased aunt Maude down the road."

Jameson chuckled softly and nodded. "It sure did. Maude disturbed her nest and, well, mothers don't take too kindly to people who mess up their hard work."

"That makes sense," Melanie nodded. "Is aunt Maude scared of birds?"

"Yes, Maude is scared of birds," Jameson smirked. "That and a few other things. How about we make her a birdhouse so she doesn't disturb any more nests accidentally. And you'll get the credit you need for your project."

"Ok," Melanie said begrudgingly. She normally loved sitting on the porch with her father as he created beautiful works of art with his hands, but today her thoughts were elsewhere. She couldn't help but think of the conversation she had overheard this morning between her mother and Maude at church. Opal had not joined them at church and Maude had admitted that when she walked over to Opal's house the night before, no one was home. Opal's car had been in the driveway that morning before church, but no one had come to the door when Maude knocked. Neither of them had seen Opal since Friday afternoon.

"I told you I got a bad feeling about this," Maude whispered to Ruby who was sitting in the pew in front of her gathering up her purse and cardigan.

"Opal goes on adventures all the time," Ruby reminded her. "She and aunt Willie probably went on an adventure together. They were going to some appointment in the canoe or whatnot."

"No, this feels like something different," Maude frowned. "I knocked on her door this morning and everything. She doesn't ignore me. Honestly, I ignore her half the time and she just barges on in any way. Oh Lord, Ruby, what if she's keeled over in the floor!"

"You don't think!" Ruby gasped. "Should we call someone?"

"I'm afraid to call the loony bin because once they get her they won't let her out," Maude bit her lip. "I guess we better go on over there and try again."

"I'll meet you over there as soon as Jameson finishes counting the tithe," Ruby said.

"You can always ride behind me," Maude shrugged.

Ruby's face turned an ashy shade of gray at the mere thought of riding on Maude's motorcycle. "I'd rather arrive in one piece," she replied.

The moment that Jameson was finished, he followed a worried looking Ruby and Melanie to the car. With the way that Maude drove, she was probably already at Opal's house storming the porch. Ruby silently prayed that Opal would be home in her sundress and that nothing was wrong. "She probably just overslept," Ruby mumbled to herself.

"I'm sure everything's fine," Jameson said soothingly. "She probably drank some of her aunt's latest potion and turned into Rip Van Winkle." He winked at Melanie who was watching them both in the rearview mirror.

True as predicted, Maude was on Opal's porch with her arms crossed over her chest. Opal's car was not in the driveway which seemed to irritate Maude more than no one coming to the door.

"Well, at least she isn't keeled over on the floor," Ruby pointed out.

"That heifer did ignore me this morning," Maude scowled. "I wish we could put a tracker on her. One of these days they'll invent something like that where one person can find someone else in the blink of an eye."

"I would hope not," Ruby said. "That sounds

creepy and invasive."

"It sounds necessary for some folks. Folks like Opal Tyler. I swear!" Maude huffed again. "Where could she be?"

"Well, how about I take us all back to the Manor for some tomato sandwiches. A client brought me a basket full of Slocumb tomatoes on Friday and there's nothing better than a good old tomato and mayonnaise sandwich. We can worry about Opal from the comforts of a nice front porch," Jameson offered.

"Ok," Ruby and Maude agreed.

Once lunch was over and the women retired to the living room, Jameson and Melanie sat on the front steps and began work on their birdhouse. "What's on your mind?" Jameson asked the pensive young girl.

"Mama's sure worried about aunt Opal. So is aunt Maude," Melanie said plainly.

"I'm sure Opal's fine as wine," Jameson assured her. "She's just got a lot on her mind right now."

"Like the war?" Melanie asked.

"Like the war," Jameson sighed. "Should we maybe make her a birdhouse, too?"

"I think so," Melanie nodded. "That might make her feel better."

Jameson smiled at his daughter and began shaping the pieces of wood for the perfect birdhouse. Melanie spent the next few minutes picking out what colors each birdhouse would need to be painted to perfectly suit the owner.

Meanwhile in the living room of Magnolia Manor, Maude and Ruby were trying to figure out where Opal had scampered off to.

"I'm drawing the line at calling Nadine," Maude said furiously. Ruby had merely mentioned Nadine's name and the Ladies Auxiliary and that perhaps Opal was working with Nadine on a project. "You're in the blasted club and they wouldn't be doing something without your knowledge. Plus Opal knows I can't stand Nadine and she wouldn't go off with her without letting me know."

"Opal and Nadine get along just fine," Ruby said.

Maude rolled her eyes and continued to pace the floor. "I already phoned aunt Willy and she said Opal wasn't with her. At least that's what I think she said. She was going on and on about the spiritual realm and how no one is ever really in one place and I had to hang up the phone. She sure is a special one," Maude shuddered.

"The only other option is to ride the roads looking for her," Ruby shrugged. The front door opened and they heard someone enter the front foyer. It was probably Melanie who needed yet another cookie while she helped her father outside.

"We don't know all of Opal's hiding places. She could be anywhere. Literally anywhere," Maude exclaimed.

"Are we playing hide and seek and I forgot?" Opal asked.

"Ahhh!" Maude shrieked. "Where did you come from?"

"My mother," Opal shrugged. "You know how

all that works. When two people love each other," she began, but Ruby cut her off. "Opal! Where have you been? We've been so worried!"

"Sorry about that," Opal nodded. "I've been busy doing things and needed some time." Opal had a way about her that was matter of fact when she didn't want to further explain herself.

"Anything we can help with?" Ruby offered.

"I don't think so," Opal said quickly. She glanced over her shoulder and then sat on the couch. "Why are y'all staring at me?"

"Because we've been worried about you!" Ruby exclaimed. "Maude practically beat your front door down and everything."

Opal yawned and then reached for her purse that had fallen to her feet. She pulled out what looked like a piece of candy and unwrapped it. "Want one?" she offered Ruby and Maude.

"I learned a long time ago not to eat anything from your purse," Maude shook her head.

"It's pure honey," Opal said. "Suit yourself."

"Opal Clementine Tyler, where the hell have you been?" Maude demanded.

Opal took a deep breath and tucked her legs underneath her. "I want to make a difference in the world and, well, sometimes that means taking a stand."

"What exactly does that mean?" Maude asked.

"I've been at a meeting," Opal said blankly. "They're talking about a demonstration."

"Oh Opal," Ruby said gently.

"It's not like those we've seen on tv," Opal shook her head. "This was will be in front of the governor's mansion telling him to stop sending our men, our boys, and hell, our women, all our people over there."

"Over to Vietnam?" Maude asked. "I thought you supported the soldiers?"

"It's not that we don't support our friends and family or our military, but we can't keep supporting this," Opal continued. "It's not right. It's just not right." She wiped a tear from the corner of her eye and looked up to see her two friends listening intently.

"I understand," Maude said. "I think."

"What are you hoping to accomplish?" Ruby asked.

"No more dying, no more deaths. No more men returned in body bags or with pieces of them missing," Opal said with vigor. "Y'all don't see what I see down at the VA or under the bridges in Montgomery or Birmingham. It's not right."

"What are you doing under the bridges?" Maude asked.

"Feeding our veterans who have nowhere else to go. They live there, under the bridges and by the river. Aunt Willy took me there Friday and I met a whole group of them. Oh God, y'all, some of them are just kids. Beat up and broken and hiding from things they can't even see. Running every time a frog croaks or a boat motor backfires. I've never seen anything like this," Opal whispered.

"That's so awful," Ruby said. She moved over to the couch and held Opal's hand. "How can we help?"

"I don't know," Opal said. "I don't even know

how I can help. I just listened while these men talked and handed out food and medicine with aunt Willy. That's where she goes every weekend."

"Why didn't you tell us?" Maude asked.

"I don't know," Opal said. "It's a lot to take in. It's a lot to experience. I don't even know what I'm doing."

"Are you going back next weekend?" Maude asked.

Opal nodded. The front door opened and Melanie came inside holding a roughly hewn birdhouse. "Look mama! We made a birdhouse. Daddy's making another right now for me to paint later."

"I love it!" Ruby exclaimed. She stood up and hugged her daughter and took the birdhouse from Melanie. "This is the best birdhouse I've ever seen. Thank you!"

"Aunt Opal, are you home now?" Melanie asked. "I thought you maybe ran away."

"Yes, Melly, I'm home. I would never run away from any of you. Do you any Jameson need help with the birdhouse?" Opal asked.

"Yes ma'am!" Melanie said excitedly. She pulled Opal by the hand back outside to the porch where Jameson was bent over a pile of wood.

"Solve all the world's problems in there?" Jameson grinned.

"Working on it," Opal smiled.

"Blue or green?" Melanie asked. "I want to make my mama one, too, that's white and yellow to match the magnolias over there. Aunt Maude likes green, right? Do you want blue?"

"That would be lovely," Opal smiled.

"There's plenty of paint in the shed," Jameson gestured to the shed by the back gate. "Why don't y'all see if the right shade of paint is in there."

"Let's go!" Melanie squealed. She jogged to the shed and beckoned Opal to follow her.

"You don't have to save the whole world alone you know," Jameson whispered to Opal. "You've got family and friends who can help you."

"I know," Opal smiled. "Thanks." She followed behind Melanie and helped the youngster rifle through various tools and cans of paint before she was satisfied. She found a small can of periwinkle blue and another can of dark green. "These will be perfect!" Melanie delighted. "Now where is one for mama?"

Opal used the small ladder to climb a little higher to see the top shelves. She found a large can of white paint, but couldn't find any shade of yellow in the entire shed. After a few seconds of internal debating, Melanie agreed that a plain white birdhouse would still be perfect.

It didn't take them long to paint the first birdhouse white. As soon as Jameson finished another house, Melanie quickly slathered it with paint. Once all three houses were formed and painted, Jameson placed them near the magnolia tree to dry. There didn't seem to be any storms on the horizon that would interfere in the drying process. He knew that Melanie didn't have the patience to wait very long for her beloved projects. He promised her that they would be ready in time for her next scouts meeting after school on Friday.

"I've got plenty of tomatoes left for a nice big salad this evening," Jameson said once they were all back inside the house.

"That sounds nice," Ruby agreed. "Opal? Maude? How does that sound?"

"You know I don't like rabbit food," Maude frowned. She lit up a cigarette, took a long drag, and blew the smoke out of her mouth. "But I could make some more tomato and mayonnaise sandwiches."

"Maude, you ought to give up smoking. I keep telling you. You know there's a reason they've been banned from advertising on the radio and television," Opal sighed.

"They're my one vice in life," Maude shrugged. Opal rolled her eyes, but she knew when to let it go. "Are we having tomato sandwiches or not?"

"Does that not count as rabbit food?" Opal asked.

"Have you ever seen a rabbit make a sandwich? I didn't think so," Maude retorted.

"If they had them some of these Slocumb tomatoes they just might," Jameson teased. "Alright, a nice big salad and some tomato sandwiches for supper. Can't go wrong with some sweet tea either."

"Too bad we ate all of that lemon loaf the other day," Maude said.

"Lemon and tomatoes? All that acid is not good for your stomach," Opal winced.

"My stomach is just fine. It's like an iron tank," Maude shrugged.

"More like an old goat," Opal chuckled.

While, Melanie showered, Jameson got to work on his salad. Ruby sliced tomatoes for anyone who wanted sandwiches. Maude stirred in sugar for the sweet tea. She preferred to make the sweet tea when she could. It wasn't that she didn't trust Jameson or Ruby's measuring, but she knew just the right amount of sugar. She knew better than to let Opal make the sweet tea because Opal preferred to drink unsweet tea if it was available. She wasn't sure how Opal could ever claim to be from the south. It wasn't proper. The woman didn't like sweet tea or grits, though she wouldn't fuss if either was served. Opal was a strange bird, but Maude would throat punch anyone else who ever said so. That's what friends were for.

"This may be the best salad I've ever seen," Jameson showed off his work. A heaping pile of lettuce, cucumbers, tomatoes, onions, and carrots glistened in the Ruby's glass salad bowl.

"You forgot the bread," Maude said.

"Seasoned croutons at your service," Jameson said as he sprinkled the crusty bits over the top.

"I thought you weren't eating salad anyway?" Opal mused. "Salad would actually be good for you. Especially, with all the acid and other junk you got going on in there. I can hear that thing rumbling from a mile away."

"Why is it that when we're together we always end up talking about Maude's body parts functioning?" Ruby gagged.

"I don't want to know," Jameson said plugging his ears. The conversation was saved as Melanie entered the kitchen with her straight black hair still wet from the shower. "Let's eat!"

"Yea, best not to spoil dinner with talks of Maude's colon," Opal agreed.

Chapter Eight

The old adage about April showers generally held true in Rhinestone. The spring showers usually rolled in every afternoon like clockwork after a day of sunshine. One Saturday morning in Rhinestone, a sunny spring day heralded the awakening of the town's natural beauty and Southern charm. As the first light of dawn filtered through the ancient oaks that lined Magnolia Manor, casting dappled shadows on the manicured lawn and blooming azalea bushes, the air was infused with the delicate fragrance of a flowering magnolia in full bloom. The estate, with its graceful antebellum architecture and sprawling garden stood as a testament to the town's rich history and genteel hospitality.

On a normal spring day in the heart of Rhinestone, locals liked to gather at the town square, where the oak trees provided shade for the quaint shops and cafes that lined the streets. Old friends exchanged warm greetings, while children laughed and played under the watchful gaze of their parents. The sound of church bells drifted on the gentle breeze, a reminder of the town's close-knit community and deep-rooted traditions. Rhinestone was the safest place in all of America, at least that what everyone who lived there proudly boasted. There wasn't much crime in the town, though its close proximity to Junction, a much larger city, sometimes allowed hooligans to cross the boundaries into the town's inner sanctuary.

At Magnolia Manor itself, the home of the Montgomery family, the morning unfolded in peaceful serenity. The sun bathed the steps of the front porch and white columns in a golden glow, illuminating the rocking chairs and a large porch swing that invited guests to linger and enjoy the view of the sprawling grounds. Inside, the scent of freshly brewed coffee mingled with the aroma of freshly baked buttermilk biscuits. Melanie sat at the breakfast table with her parents discussing her goal to sell the most Girl Scout cookies which was proving difficult because she had started in the Scouts later than most of the other girls. Still she was determined. Later that evening an idea struck her like electricity. She knew exactly who to go to. Maude Cooper had the biggest sweet tooth out of anyone she knew. Once Melanie showed Maude the list of available boxes of cookies, her job was done. Maude quickly scooped them all up and loaded them in the trunk of Opal's car.

"Easiest project she's ever completed," Ruby chuckled.

"Those should last her a week, maybe less," Jameson shrugged playfully.

True to his prediction, Maude walked into the Manor holding her last box of peanut butter cookies the following weekend to discuss what was on everyone's mind.

"It's disgusting, that's what it is," Maude shook with fury. "They killed them in cold blood for what? There wasn't any rhyme or reason for what they did. And they call themselves a family? That's ridiculous! Ain't no family, just a bunch of crazies. It ain't right."

Maude, Ruby, and Opal had been glued to the television in March when the penalty phase of the trial concluded for the infamous Manson Family. The jury had announced the penalty as death for all four Tate-LaBianca defendants. Now a month later, Judge Older sentenced Charles Manson to death. Manson was sent to San Quenton's death row where he would await his execution. Maude was all for returning to hangings on the courthouse lawn, but Opal shook her head and said that wouldn't solve anything. Nothing was going to bring the gorgeous Sharon Tate or her beloved friends back to life. It was a tragedy that had rocked the nation to its core.

The Tate-LaBianca murders, orchestrated by the Manson Family in August 1969, remained one of the most infamous and chilling episodes in American criminal history. Led by Charles Manson, a charismatic but deeply disturbed figure, the Manson Family was a cult-like group that espoused apocalyptic beliefs and practiced a mix of hedonism, drug use, and quasi-communal living on the outskirts of Los Angeles, California. In early August 1969, Charles Manson ordered a group of his followers, including Tex Watson,

Susan Atkins, Patricia Krenwinkel, and Linda Kasabian to carry out a series of murders. Their primary targets were chosen seemingly at random: actress Sharon Tate, who was eight months pregnant, and her friends who were at her home that night, as well as Leno and Rosemary LaBianca, a couple killed the following night. The murders were shockingly brutal and symbolic, reflecting Manson's twisted ideology and desire to incite a race war he called "Helter Skelter" after the Beatles song. Sharon Tate, along with four others at her residence, was brutally stabbed and shot multiple times. The words "pig" and other messages were scrawled in blood at the crime scenes, intended to mislead investigators into believing the murders were committed by political radicals. The subsequent investigation and trial exposed the Manson Family's inner workings and the profound psychological hold Manson had over his followers. Manson himself did not participate directly in the killings but was convicted of orchestrating them and sentenced to death because of it. Jameson didn't believe that the death sentences would be upheld. Being a lawyer allowed him insight into the finer details that most of the public weren't privy to. There was a stirring sense of moral obligation and ethics that was growing in places like Washington D.C. and California, to which Jameson surmised that the death penalty would soon be overturned. That supposition infuriated Maude who considered herself a true crime junkie. Even though Opal teased her that she should have gone to law school, Maude said she preferred to have attended the old wild west school of hard knocks. She was into vigilante justice and no one could convince her otherwise.

"That mess wouldn't last one second in Rhinestone," Maude gritted her teeth. "Not one second at all."

"She's right," Jameson said. He turned off the television and shook his head. "It sure is a shame the awful things that people do to one another. That's all the news seem to show these days." He kissed Ruby on the top of her head and walked upstairs.

"This case has been rough on him hasn't it?" Opal asked.

"It has," Ruby nodded. "Thankfully, he's never had to defend anyone like those people. I can't imagine something like that."

"Do you think something like that could ever happen in Rhinestone?" Maude asked.

"You just said it wouldn't," Opal reminded her.

"I know, but I guess it could," Maude shuddered.

"I don't even want to think about that," Ruby said.

"He's right though. People do such awful things to each other. I see it in those men every time I go down there by the river," Opal breathed.

"War is hell. Isn't that what they say," Maude nodded.

"Yea, well, if everyone saw what I've seen, there wouldn't be any more war ever again," Opal sighed.

"Yea," Ruby nodded. Opal had invited her to go with her and aunt Willy the next time they brought food and medicine to the encampment, but she nor Maude was sure they could go. She remembered the way her uncle Woodrow, her mother's baby brother, had been after he came home from France from World War II. She remembered the times that he would hide underneath the porch anytime a truck backfired. There were days when he was super pleasant and kind, but after he had been drinking for days on end, he would become skittish and disappear for days. One afternoon he killed himself in the middle of a cornfield. She had never thought it possible, but this war in Vietnam was turning out to be even worse than the world wars that had come before. "Let's change the subject." She wrapped her cardigan around her arms and shivered.

"I've been thinking about this question for a bit," Opal said. "If you could have one super power, what would it be?"

"Really? That's what you've been thinking about?" Maude rolled her eyes.

"Yes, I'd want to heal people," Opal said seriously.

"Ooh, I don't know," Ruby said. "What are the options?"

"Anything!" Opal answered.

"Like being invisible or turning anything to gold or flying," Maude revealed.

"You can only pick one," Opal reminded her.

"I'll turn everything into gold!" Maude sputtered quickly. She looked rather pleased with herself.

"Everything you touch turns to gold?" Opal asked questioningly.

"We'd all be rich!" Maude nodded.

"No, we'd all be gold statues," Opal pointed out. "You are like a kid in a candy store. You can't help but touch everything. We'll be walking in the Pig and you've gotta run your grubby little fingers over everything."

Maude threw a pillow at Opal who caught it before it knocked over the lamp on the end table. "See! This would be a golden pillow. And the couch you're sitting on. And your purse. And your glass of sweet tea. And your pillow at night."

"I get it! Geez!" Maude interrupted her. "Then maybe I'd be invisible."

"So you can watch people in the shower? Absolutely not!" Opal chided. Ruby giggled and shook her head. "That would be odd," she agreed.

"Why do you always have to make things so awkward!" Maude shouted. "Then flying is my only option!"

"Hope you're a better flier than you are a driver," Opal giggled.

Maude rolled her eyes again and stared at Ruby waiting for her to make her declaration. "Oh, um, I guess I would like to either heal people or be able to point my finger and turn something into food so I could feed people," Ruby mused.

"I'd like to change mine to pointing my finger at someone and turning them into a moose," Maude said.

"Like this?" Opal asked. She narrowed her

eyebrows and pointed her finger at Maude before making a weird whittling sound between her teeth.

"Stop that!" Maude howled. She didn't think that Opal had the power to turn her into a mammoth animal, but she wouldn't put anything past Opal. Even though Opal Tyler was her best friend in the entire world, she had to admit that Opal was wild and did scare her a little.

"It's about time I headed home anyway," Opal said. "I've got some more letters to write before the mail goes out tomorrow." She set the pillow she had been holding back in Maude's chair and gathered up the empty tea glasses to take them to the kitchen sink. "I'll see y'all soon. Tell Melanie once she's ready to get her nature badge I'll take her out in the woods to gather some herbs and flowers. We may even find a few bugs for my garden."

"As long as she keeps those bugs to herself," Maude shivered. She waved goodbye to Ruby and followed Opal outside to their respective vehicles. Ruby watched them both leave down the driveway and turn onto the highway. Melanie was due home any minute from her grandmother's house. Ruby's parents lived twenty minutes away from Magnolia Manor and Melanie loved to spend time with her grandmother and granddaddy. She often returned home with a new toy from their shopping adventures or a Tupperware bin full of cookies they had baked.

Ruby's father, John, was a history professor at the local community college. Ruby's mother,

Barbara, had retired from teaching middle school and enjoyed spending time with her grandchildren. Melanie loved running around outside with her cousins, the children of Ruby's older brother, when they came to visit. Ruby's brother was a minister who traveled all over the world preaching the gospel with his wife. Ruby's older sister had passed away when Ruby was fifteen from medical complications that she had been born with. Ruby missed her sister, but now that she was a parent herself, she had a newfound respect and admiration for her own parents who worked every day to survive the death of one of their children.

Melanie was lucky in the fact that she had both sets of her grandparents nearby. Jameson was an only child, which meant that Melanie was extra spoiled by her paternal grandparents. Bertram Montgomery was a wealthy attorney in Junction who owned his own firm. Jameson has started his career at his father's office with hopes of one day opening his own firm. Jameson's mother had always been a strict woman, but grandchildren had a way of changing your heart. She loved spending time with her only grandchild and fully supported her son and daughter in law.

Ruby would never forget the day that Melanie was born. Melanie arrived two days after her due date in late January with jet black hair and piercing blue eyes. She was spoiled rotten between grandparents and friends of the family from the moment she was brought home. Melanie was a very colicky baby and would have screaming fits that lasted well into the night. Even Opal's tried and true home remedies wouldn't work every time. As Melanie grew up, she became more easygoing, but it was difficult for the two young parents not to spoil the precocious little girl.

Ruby's thoughts were interrupted by the sound of her father's pick-up truck parking next to the magnolia tree. Jameson walked downstairs and looked out the window, turned to Ruby, and smiled. "The other two Stone Sisters already head on home?"

"They left about twenty minutes ago. I'm thinking I can make some biscuits and some tomato gravy with the rest of those tomatoes for supper. How does that sound?" Ruby asked.

"Nothing ever sounded better," Jameson agreed as Melanie bounded inside carrying a cake wrapped in plastic. "What do you have there?"

"Grandma and I made a carrot cake," Melanie grinned. She shared the same sweet tooth that her daddy did. Carrot cake was their current favorite, especially paired with a scoop or two of vanilla ice cream.

Ruby's parents walked inside a few minutes later with Melanie's backpack and a shopping bag full of clothes that they had bought for Melanie. Ruby asked her parents if they would like to stay for supper, and they agreed. No one in Alabama could turn down Slocomb tomatoes.

After a filling supper of homemade biscuits and tomato gravy, topped off with homemade carrot cake and vanilla ice cream, the grownups retired to the living room while Melanie went upstairs to get ready for bed. When Melanie came downstairs, she hugged her grandparents goodbye, and they drove back to their house. Jameson and Ruby tucked their daughter into her bed and then got ready for bed themselves. Ruby sat up in bed, grading a few more essays from her students, while Jameson read over a case that went to trial on Monday.

"We've got it pretty good here in Rhinestone don't we?" Ruby asked, still focused on the stack of papers in her lap.

"We sure do," Jameson nodded. "We sure do."

Chapter Nine

"I know what I'm doing! I don't need your help," Maude huffed. She stuck her tongue out and put up her hand to hold Opal away. She was over thirty years old and didn't need anyone to hold her hand during a child's arts and crafts time. No wonder all the girls kept looking over at her. Opal wouldn't stop pestering her or Melanie.

"I never said you needed my help," Opal sassed. "You need serious professional help that I am unable to provide."

All ten heads had turned to look at the two women who were squabbling. The young girls had long foregone their own crafts at the sight of the circus in front of them. "Is there a problem over here?" the woman in charge of the craft project asked.

Maude glared over the young woman's shoulder to shoot Opal a dirty look. "Everything is fine," she grimaced. "I know what paste is, for God's sake," Maude muttered under her breath.

"I just thought I saw her tasting the paste," Opal whispered to the lady.

"The paste? Oh no ma'am," the lady howled. "Even my young ladies know not to eat the paste.

If this continues, I'm afraid I'm going to have to ask you to leave the room."

To Opal's immense surprise, Maude held her tongue and swallowed back the curse words that had risen up in her throat. "Yes ma'am," she breathed. Opal chuckled underneath her breath and winked at Melanie who was sitting next to Maude. The little girl giggled as Opal walked back to her table that she was volunteering with. Maude noticed the grin on her face and shook her head. "I wasn't eating paste," she whispered. "Opal was the one who ate it when we were kids. I always knew better."

"Yes ma'am," Melanie nodded. She couldn't imagine how anyone would eat this thick glob of paste that smelled funny. She frowned slightly at the mess of popsicle sticks and globs of paste on the table in front of her. "I can't get the sticks to act right."

"I think you've got too much glue going on," Maude mused. She brushed a strand of hair out of her eyes and bent over her own project. The group was supposed to be making picture frames out of small wooden sticks from the local craft store, but the glue was proving difficult for some of the girls.

"Um, Maude," Opal began.

"Shh," Maude hissed. She flung the piece of her hair out of her eye again and bent over the jumbled heap of sticks on the table in front of her. She wiped her hands on her pants and then scratched her chin. "I think I have too much glue here."

"You think?" Opal snickered. "Bless your

heart!"

"Huh?" Maude asked as Opal continued to laugh. "There's still plenty of paste to go around. Y'all need any over yonder?" She gestured to the table nearest her and frowned slightly as the young girls giggled and shook their heads.

"Maude, we're gonna have to wash your hair something fierce to get all that paste out," Opal cackled. "You've got more on you than you do the sticks!"

Maude frowned and tried to shake the thick paste out of her hair. "I don't know why you had to go and put paste in my hair," she huffed.

"You did that all by yourself," Opal pointed out. "Don't go blaming anyone but you."

"Do you like my picture frame?" Melanie asked. Opal dabbed a bit of the paste that was dripping off and smiled widely. "It's absolutely perfect. What picture are you going to put in it once it dries?" she asked.

"I think one of Ginger Belle, my cat," Melanie nodded.

"Ginger Belle?" Maude asked. "What is a Ginger Belle?"

"My kitten that lives in the barn!" Melanie smiled.

"Which one is Ginger Belle?" Maude asked. Melanie was always bringing home a new stray so it was hard to keep track.

"The orange one, of course! It lives in the barn with Flutterby and Willow," Melanie explained.

"Flutterby? Willow? God, you must get your naming ability from Opal. I swear she comes up with the most random names for things," Maude rolled her eyes.

"I think those are lovely names," Opal smiled. "Unlike Maude, I like to have a little creativity when I name things. Unlike Maude who keeps the same name for every single pet she's ever had."

"It makes life easier," Maude shrugged. "That way you don't have to learn a new name."

"If you ever have children, are you just going to name them after yourself or keep the dog's name?" Opal asked.

"God, I hope I never have children," Maude countered. Every young girl's head quickly turned toward her with their eyes wide. "Well, um, not that there's anything wrong with having children," she swallowed. She turned to Opal and hissed, "Dammit Opal, you did that on purpose. You know I'm not good with kids. I only like one or two." She put her arm around Melanie and squeezed the young girl in a hug.

Melanie giggled and gathered up her book bag and blew on her picture frame. She couldn't wait to show her parents once she got home. Jameson and Ruby were at a dinner with some people from Jameson's office. Opal had volunteered to take Melanie to her weekly meeting and Maude had tagged along. Melanie secretly hoped that Maude and Opal would be able to take her to more meetings in the future. They always made her laugh.

"What time will Jameson and Ruby be done?" Maude asked.

"Not for another hour or so, I expect," Opal

answered.

"Great! That means we have time for ice cream," Maude suggested.

"We have to have dinner first," Opal said.

"Ice cream is dinner," Maude shrugged. Melanie clapped her hands and hurried to Opal's car. She never said no to ice cream, especially ice cream for dinner.

Opal shrugged and nodded in agreement. "Ice cream it is! If Ruby gets upset, it's your fault, Maude," she added.

Maude rolled her eyes and began thinking about what ice cream her stomach felt like. When they pulled into the parking lot of Dixie's Dairy Delights, the oldest ice cream shop in the county, Maude made a beeline for the door. "We better hurry or she'll eat all the ice cream on her own," Opal winked at Melanie.

"I'll take the triple decker sundae with an extra scoop of chocolate. Extra whipped cream. And extra sprinkles, the chocolate sprinkles," Maude told the high school boy behind the counter. His eyes widened in surprise and asked how many spoons she would need.

"Oh, you think she's going to share?" Opal giggled. "That's cute. Nope, that's all for her. Now as for me, I'll have the double scoop of strawberry in a bowl. Melanie? What would you like?"

"A hot fudge sundae, please," Melanie smiled.

A few minutes later the boy brought over their order and set the massive dish of ice cream in front of Maude. "If you eat it all in twenty minutes or less, you win a pint of vanilla ice cream," he mumbled.

"Easy," Maude said with a grin.

Melanie and Opal ate their ice cream slowly as they watched Maude quickly work her way through the ten scoops of various ice creams in the glass dish in front of her. The bottom layer had three scoops of chocolate ice cream topped with a drizzle of chocolate fudge sauce. The middle layer had three scoops of vanilla ice cream with sprinkles. The top layer had three scoops of strawberry ice cream with whipped cream. Maude's extra scoop of chocolate topped with extra sprinkles and whipped cream had been delivered in a separate dish, but Maude had devoured that almost immediately.

"Is she ok?" the teenager asked Opal as Maude began tackling the bottom layer of ice cream that had all but drowned in the hot fudge sauce.

"No, she's pretty feral when it comes to ice cream," Opal shrugged. "Very deranged, but as long as you don't get in her way, she won't hurt you."

"Um, ok," he stuttered and backed away slowly.

"Anyway, Melanie, what was your leader saying about your service project for next week?" Opal asked.

Melanie took another large mouthful of her ice cream sundae and smiled brightly at Opal. "We can do any sort of thing, but my teacher suggested that we interview someone old and learn more about the history of Rhinestone. She wants us to connect with the older generations."

"Oh, that sounds great. You should definitely interview Maude because she is a treasure trove of information and definitely fits the old criteria," Opal grinned.

Maude wiped her mouth with the back of her hand and burped loudly. "That was delicious! How'd I do?" She waved her hand at the teenage boy who was behind the counter and his jaw dropped. "You finished it?" he asked incredulously.

"Of course I did," Maude said.

He checked his watch and gasped. "That's a new record! That's a Dixie record for sure! Nine and a half minutes," he choked.

"I'm surprised it took that long," Opal whispered to Melanie.

"You got any coffee?" Maude asked. "I need something to counteract this cold from the ice cream."

"No ma'am," the boy shook his head. "Do you want your free pint now or when you go?"

"I think we're ready to go now, please," Opal said. There was no way Maude would be able to stomach any more ice cream. She may be feeling fine now, but she was going to be feeling all of that dairy delight in a few hours and Opal did not want to be anywhere near it. "Alright, let's get you home, Mel!"

Maude cradled her free pint of vanilla ice cream in her lap a few minutes later and moaned quietly in the front seat. "Don't drive so fast," she hiccupped to Opal.

"Starting to feel it, huh?" Opal asked as they turned into the driveway of Magnolia Manor.

"Maybe a little," Maude hiccupped again. She exited the car before Opal had fully come to a stop. Jameson and Ruby hadn't arrived back yet, but she had a key to the Manor and Opal could help Melanie bring in her art project.

The next afternoon the Ladies Auxiliary met in Belle's living room to discuss ideas for the fundraiser. They needed something that would not only be entertaining, but would bring in a lot of money. Many people threw out the idea of a bake sale. While a bake sale would certainly sound delicious, they didn't think it would bring in the necessary money that they would need. A community wide yard sale had the same problem. There were plenty of people who were willing to donate their used items for the yard sale, just as there were plenty of women who would love to bake for the bake sale, but they needed a quick way to raise a lot of money. Patsy suggested they hold a talent show, but they quickly realized that not many of them had the talent to pull that off. Selling tickets to a mediocre talent show would end up costing them more time and money in the long run. Nadine wanted to have a beauty pageant, but her idea was quickly shot down. That sounded like more drama and effort than any of them had time for.

"What we need is a game show! Or a telethon!" Opal suggested.

"Wow, a telethon!" Patsy agreed. "That could work!"

"How would we even go about doing that?" Nadine had perked up instantly at the idea. The group went quiet before Ruby suggested working with the local news to see if they could donate some of their air time and people could volunteer manning the telephones.

"We could do it live and update the total amount of money raised. We would need some entertaining acts to entertain viewers. That way we could also accept donations in person," Nadine continued.

"This sounds like a lot of work," Maude coughed from the corner. She still refused to join the group, but Opal and Ruby insisted that she accompany them to the meeting before they all had dinner afterwards. Nadine cut her eyes at Maude, but she had to admit that the grumpy woman was right. It was going to be a huge undertaking.

"You'll need a host," Maude uttered.

"She's right," Nadine said with a sigh. "I think we should take a vote."

"What about you, Opal?" Ruby suggested.

"Yeah, Opal would be great!" Maude agreed.

Opal shook her head. "I don't want to be the host. I want to be the talent."

"The talent?" Belle asked.

"Yes, and I want to be the assistant that showcases the different prizes and collect the money," Opal said in a fake British accent.

"Now we have to think about prizes," Ruby grimaced. "How would we go about that? Maybe do a raffle for people who donate? If you donate a certain amount then you get entered to win the grand prize. Oh goodness, I don't even know."

"I think we're going to need another meeting,"

Lulu sighed.

By the end of the meeting, Nadine was elected the host of the telethon and Opal was going to be her assistant. Ruby knew that the matter had not been settled on what Opal's outfit would be. If she knew her like she thought she did, she knew that Opal would probably have multiple costume changes throughout the event.

"Y'all didn't even talk about food," Maude said as she slid into the chair at Ruby's dining room table.

"What do we need food for?" Opal asked.

"You gotta have a catering table or something said. I can be in charge of that," Maude explained.

"Nobody wants your cooking!" Opal reminded her.

"I didn't say I was going to cook. I said I can be in charge, like being security for the food. You don't want all those random people to just be standing around. You gotta give them something to do. You gotta keep their spirits up. Gotta make sure they stay healthy," Maude continued.

"You wouldn't know healthy if it bit you in the butt," Opal cackled.

"Y'all quit," Ruby shook her head. "I've got to get this chicken in the oven before Jameson and Melanie get back. Maude, help me with this, please. Opal, can you start on the salad?"

"Of course, Ruby," Opal said dutifully.

"Jameson's going to ask about dessert," Ruby laughed under her breath. "Opal, how's that peach cobbler look? Mr. and Mrs. Harrison gave it to us last night."

"Looks fine to me. We can top it off with some of Maude's vanilla ice cream she left in your freezer last night," Opal suggested.

"I think I'll skip the ice cream for now," Maude muttered.

"It must have been bad for you to swear off ice cream," Ruby said with her eyebrows raised.

"Don't ask," Maude grumbled.

"Dixie's Dairy Delights will never be the same," Opal giggled.

Chapter Ten

No one was quite sure how to prepare for a telethon of this size, probably because none of them had ever witnessed a telethon of any size before. Ruby and Nadine ran all over town whenever they weren't at work making sure everything and everyone was staying on schedule. Lulu had been put in charge of securing sponsors, but that quickly became overwhelming, so she recruited Ellen to help her. Before long, the Ladies Auxiliary had been presented with quite a few very nice raffle items for their event. Even Maude pitched in when Nadine swerved to miss a deer that she swore jumped out in front of her by getting her tires realigned and her brakes replaced in a jiffy. Nadine tapped her foot impatiently the entire time which made Maude grimace more and sigh louder than ever. Nadine kept reminding her that she was on a very tight schedule, not that Maude was dallying; she wanted to get Nadine in and out as quickly as possible.

Opal, on the other hand, knew that her contribution as the talent portion of the show required the strictest schedule of all. She was up every morning before dawn to do her morning calisthenics as the morning sun rose overhead. She topped off her morning exercise with a quick mile run down the lane and back before many of her neighbors were awake. Later in the afternoon she made time to practice her routines. She wasn't quite certain how much air time she would have, but she needed to be ready for any and everything. Live television was difficult to plan for, but she would be ready.

As the telethon neared, everyone's anxiety started to run high. Opal offered to make everyone one of her infamous teas that she swore would help reduce their nerves and restore calm, but no one took her up on her offer, much to her dismay. Rather than get upset, Opal decided to encourage everyone to continue to get the word out about the event however they could. Patsy's husband wrote a moving article in the Rhinestone Register titled "The Telethon of Friendship: A Community's Call."

"In the small town of Rhinestone, nestled between rolling hills and surrounded by rich forests, a tight-knit community thrives. The heart of Rhinestone was its church, Beaver Crossing Holy Church for the Faithful, which had been a gathering place for generations. With its wooden steeple reaching towards the sky and stained glass window telling a story of faith, it had witnessed weddings, baptisms, and countless community events. However, in recent years, the church has faced financial challenges. The roof needed fixing, the back steps needed replacing, and there was no place to baptize the sinners of the world besides the cow trough outside.

As the women of the congregation gathered one Sunday morning, an idea was sparked. There had to be a way to raise the necessary funds and allow the women time together to fellowship. The newly formed Ladies Auxiliary leader, Nadine Waters, gave a few words. "We need to raise funds to keep our church thriving," she said. "We have a vision for the future, but we cannot do it alone. I'm calling on all of you to help."

Lifelong members of Beaver Crossing knew they could tackle any issue: Patsy Collins, Nadine Waters, Ruby Montgomery, Belle Wilbanks, Patricia Finnigan, Ellen Abernathy, Lucille Adams, Opal Tyler, Lulu McBride, and Leanne Humpderdink put their minds together and formed The Ladies Auxiliary, open to any woman in Rhinestone who shares their passion for community involvement and positive impact. Their first line of important business is to raise money for a baptismal at Beaver Crossing Holy Church for the Faithful. They have decided to hold a telethon to raise money for their beloved church.

The friends met at Nadine's house one afternoon, excitedly brainstorming ideas for their telethon. Nadine, an aspiring event planner, took the lead. "We need a catchy name for the event. How about 'Hope and Harmony Telethon'?" Opal Tyler, an enthusiastic performer, suggested, "We can include live performances. I can be the talent."

Ellen Abernathy, a talented artist, chimed in, "We could create a visual backdrop for the stage, maybe even include a live painting montage of the church's history and community events."

Lulu McBride was asked to help gather sponsors for the event. She added, "I can handle the raffle part of things. We need to create a buzz in the tri-county area to get as many people involved as possible." With their roles established, they began planning the telethon in earnest. They set a date for a Friday evening three weeks later, giving them enough time to organize the event and spread the word. The friends divided the tasks and set out to complete their mission."

The article went on to detail the time and place of the telethon. The women hoped that they would have an incredible turnout, but the closer to time it got, Nadine began to get restless. After a straight week of complaining every time she set foot in whatever establishment she went in, Ruby sat her down and tried to calm her down. Opal once again offered her a strong cup of tea, but Nadine again refused. Maude had gotten tired of hearing about Nadine's stress that she marched up to her and placed both hands on Nadine's shoulders and shook her. "Get yourself together! Yall don't have time for this!"

"Maude, don't hurt her!" Ruby shrieked.

"I ain't hurting her," Maude scowled. "Y'all act like this is the end all be all event and it's driving me crazy. I can't set hide nor hair anywhere without hearing about it. Nadine, it's going to be fine, but if you don't shake it off, I'm gonna have to kill you or start drinking!"

For whatever reason, Maude's sudden outburst seemed to have the best effect on Nadine's and everyone else's nerves. "She's crazy, but it does work," Opal nodded in agreement while doing Patsy's hair at the beauty salon one morning. She made a mental note to possibly spike Maude's dinner tea with some calming oils the evening of the fundraiser. Maude, who still refused to be a part of the Auxiliary, hadn't made up her mind yet whether or not she would be in physical attendance for the telethon or not. She knew that if Ruby and Opal had their say, she'd end up helping in some form or fashion. They always managed to rope her into their shenanigans.

As the remaining days ticked down, the ladies immersed themselves in preparation. They met regularly, sometimes at Nadine's house and other times at the church, where they felt the spirit of their mission guiding them.

Patsy suggested a unique fundraising strategy. "Let's set up a pledge system. People can donate a certain amount for every hour we broadcast, and we can have special incentives. For example, if we reach five hundred dollars, Opal could perform a song requested by the highest donor." The idea sparked enthusiasm, and they expanded on it. They decided to offer various levels of sponsorships for local businesses, encouraging them to contribute in exchange for advertising during the telethon. They also thought about incorporating a silent auction, where community members could donate items or services to be auctioned off live.

Ellen took charge of creating visually appealing flyers to promote the event. She crafted a compelling message that highlighted the church's history and the importance of community support. They shared the flyers in local businesses, schools, and even handed them out at grocery stores and in the line at the bank.

As the day of the telethon approached, the group worked tirelessly. Jameson had carved a beautiful podium that was sure to be used for years to come. The day before the big event, the women spent the evening decorating the school's auditorium with colorful banners and lights, creating a vibrant atmosphere. On the evening of the telethon, the hall was filled with community members eager to support their church. The air buzzed with excitement, and the scent of freshly baked goods wafted from the refreshment table. The ladies had set up one hundred chairs and every single one of them was filled.

The preacher gathered everyone present in a circle to bow in prayer before Opal warmed up the crowd with an acoustic performance. She scanned the crowd and didn't see Maude. She frowned slightly, but the show must go on. She caught Nadine out of the corner of her eye jumping for joy as the clock ticked closer to time.

"And five, four, three, two, one!" The telethon had officially began!

The bright lights of the cameras lit up the mayor as he interviewed Nadine about the formation of the Ladies Auxiliary and their mission tonight. Nadine expressed gratitude for the hard work and the community's support. "Tonight, we come together not just to raise funds but to celebrate our shared faith and commitment to one another," she said, her voice filled with emotion.

The telethon featured live performances from local musicians, and Opal played a prominent role. It was easy to see why she was so loved by everyone who knew her. She could go from singing lead on a ballad to perfectly harmonizing with the church choir. Each performance was interspersed with personal stories from congregation members, sharing how Beaver Crossing Holy Church had impacted their lives. A young couple spoke about their wedding, a family shared their experiences with the church's choir program, and an elderly man recounted how the church had been a source of comfort during the difficult time when his wife had passed away.

As the night wore on, the pledges began to pour in. People from the community called in to donate and the excitement in the room grew. The friends felt a sense of pride and accomplishment while witnessing the impact of their efforts. Midway through the event, they introduced the silent auction. Local businesses had generously donated items ranging from handmade crafts to gift certificates. Nadine took the stage and encouraged attendees to bid generously. "Remember, every dollar goes directly to our church! Let's make a difference together!"

The energy in the hall was infectious. Community members rallied to support one another, raising their hands to bid on items. Laughter filled the air as people playfully competed for their favorite items, and the friends marveled at the sense of camaraderie surrounding them.

However, not everything went smoothly. As the night progressed, the group of ladies faced unexpected challenges. Technical difficulties arose when the livestream feed faltered, causing panic among the group. Belle quickly grabbed the microphone, addressing the audience with calm confidence. "Thank you for your patience, everyone! We're experiencing some technical issues, but we'll be back shortly. In the meantime, let's keep the donations coming!"

Her words resonated with the crowd, who began cheering and chanting for the telethon to continue. The energy was palpable, and soon the technical issues were resolved. Opal jumped back on stage, dedicating a heartfelt song to the church and its community. The crowd sang along, their voices rising in unison, creating a beautiful harmony that filled the hall.

As the telethon approached its conclusion, the friends gathered backstage to review the fundraising totals. Jameson, who had been diligently tracking the donations, reported, "We've raised almost four thousand dollars so far! This is incredible!"

While the money was being totaled, the news station was able to get them back on air. Encouraged by the response, they decided to make a final push for donations. "Let's give it one last big effort," Nadine said. "We can do this!"

With renewed energy, they took the stage for the finale. Nadine addressed the crowd and the viewers on the television, "Tonight, we've witnessed the power of community. We are here not just as individuals but as a family united in faith and love. Let's make this last hour count!"

Opal stepped up to perform a new song she had written specifically for the telethon, titled "Together We Rise." The lyrics resonated deeply, capturing the spirit of their community. As she strummed the guitar and sang, the audience felt a sense of connection and hope. People began to stand and sway, joining in with claps and cheers. Even Maude who had just stuffed a piece of thick chocolate cake in her mouth was overcome with emotion.

Nadine and Belle joined Opal on stage in front of the camera, encouraging the crowd to pledge in real-time. "For every fifty dollars pledged in the next ten minutes, we'll sing a verse of this song together!" they announced.

As the clock ticked down, people rushed to call in their pledges, driven by the excitement and sense of urgency. The atmosphere was electric, and the friends felt a rush of adrenaline as they witnessed the community's overwhelming support.

As the telethon came to a close, they announced the final total. "Thanks to your incredible generosity, we raised almost five thousand dollars!" Nadine exclaimed, and the crowd erupted in applause. The friends hugged each other, tears of joy in their eyes. They had set out to make a difference, and they had succeeded beyond their expectations.

It took another hour before the crowd finally

left. The last cake had been sold as the news station packed up their equipment. Maude, Nadine, and Lulu made quick work of putting away the chairs while Ruby and Ellen swept the floor and wiped down the tables. Opal, Patsy, and Patricia helped the donors back to the cars and personally thanked everyone who had been a part of the telethon.

After everything had been cleaned and put away, the group of ladies gathered together, still buzzing from the night's success. Reverend Barton joined them, beaming with pride. "You've shown what true community looks like. This event will go down in history as a testament to your hard work and dedication."

The impact of their efforts would be felt long after the telethon ended. The funds raised would allow for Beaver Crossing Holy Church to finally install a baptismal indoors. They would even have some money left over to repair a leak in the roof and order new choir hymnals.

As Maude, Ruby, and Opal walked outside to Ruby's car, Nadine stopped them and hugged them all tightly. "And even you, Maude. You helped!" Nadine shrieked happily. Her eyes were wide and she giggled like a schoolgirl.

"Are you high?" Maude asked.

"High on life!" Nadine squeaked. "I don't think I'll be able to sleep after tonight. What a night!" She practically skipped to her car as she hummed remnants of Opal's song.

"That really was amazing," Ruby agreed. "Don't you want to officially join the Auxiliary, Maude?"

"Not a chance," Maude yawned. "Anyone want a slice of this cake before I head home?"

"I can't believe you bought an entire cake," Ruby giggled.

"Well, I didn't buy an entire cake," Maude grumbled. "I actually bought two, and I was gonna share."

"Thanks, Maude," Opal laughed. "Over the years of Rhinestone's bake sales, you've probably paid for half the stuff in this town."

"Just doing my civic duty," Maude grinned.

Chapter Eleven

In the weeks that followed, the friends reflected on their journey. What began as a simple idea had blossomed into a powerful experience that brought their community together. They realized that the telethon was not just about raising money; it was about strengthening the bonds of friendship and faith. The Ladies Auxiliary vowed to meet twice a month now that it had become so much more than simply sharing laughs and stories; they now had a mission to continue their goodwill and generosity within the community. They were all still in disbelief and how well their inaugural fundraiser had gone. They spoke about how each person in the community played a vital role in the success of the telethon. The friendships they forged during this process deepened, and they committed to continuing their work together for the church and the community. As they looked ahead, they decided to make the telethon an annual event, fostering a tradition of unity and generosity. With each passing year, they hoped to build on their success, involving more community members and expanding their outreach efforts.

As the ladies pressed on within their own

community, the rest of the world continued to spiral into chaos. The constant sadness and anxiety that swirled in the air above Rhinestone and every other city in America called for action. Maybe that's what pushed Opal over the edge. She had written thousands of letters to soldiers and to men in Washington who wore black suits and drank bottles of wine after a long day on Capitol Hill. Those kinds of letters fell on deaf ears for far too long. Her mind was made up. Her bus ticket was purchased. She would be leaving in the morning come hell or high water to do her part.

The grey skies of late spring hung heavy over Washington, D.C. on the morning of April 24th. A damp chill clung to the air, but it didn't matter. Opal Tyler, dressed in her favorite flowered blouse and denim jeans, stood at the steps of the Greyhound station, the sound of the bus's engine fading into the distance. She adjusted the weight of her canvas purse against her shoulder, her fingers brushing the edges of the small peace symbol pin she had stitched on it. The city before her looked just like it did in the magazines and on the television screen: old buildings, monuments, and the Capitol rising like a stubborn tower in the distance. But this time, it wasn't just an image on the screen or in her memory. It was real. She was really here where history was about to happen again. This time she would be a part of it.

Thousands of people had set up a makeshift camp around the bank of the Potomac River. Music filled the air from live musicians with guitars and from staticky old radios. She looked at the crowds of people already beginning to gather for the protest. They came in all shapes and sizes, from students in bell-bottoms to veterans in old uniforms, their faces weathered and angry, to middle-aged women like herself. They were all strangers to rebellion, but no longer strangers to what was happening in the world. War, loss, anger, and frustration had united them all. This protest wasn't just about the war in Vietnam anymore; it was about everything.

The weight of it all settled in her chest as she watched a group of young men in ragged uniforms pass by in various bandages for both old and new wounds. She felt a knot tighten in her stomach. What kind of world was this where young men were sent off to either die or slowly break into pieces in a far-off land for a cause they couldn't even understand? Opal wasn't one for politics. She found comfort in the little things that made life in Rhinestone worth living. But over the last two years, something had shifted inside her. Maybe it was the constant news about the war. Maybe it was the stories from her friends at the VA being drafted, some of them coming home in pieces, both physically and emotionally. Or maybe it was just the overwhelming sense that the world was turning and she didn't want to be left behind. She was a world traveler, she was cultured and open to any and everything, but something had sparked inside her. This was bigger than Rhinestone, bigger than the little salon that she dreamed of taking over one day. She felt like she had to do something. She wanted to stop being an observer every night in front of the television; she wanted to be active. So, she'd packed her bag, told her two closest friends that she was headed to a conference in North Carolina for the hair salon, and climbed onto a bus bound for D.C. She wasn't sure what exactly she was looking for. She just knew she couldn't sit back and pretend it wasn't happening.

A group of musicians noticed her walking around and waved her over. "I'm Atlas," the long-haired man with glasses smiled. "I'm Opal," she replied.

"Groovy," he nodded.

Opal was thankful to have found a spot in their group. She wasn't afraid to be alone, but it was always nicer to be included. Atlas was one of the organizers of the event. He had been there when veterans had thrown their medals onto the steps of the Capitol and when mothers had laid wreaths all around in memory of their sons who had never come back home. Together with Atlas and his friends, Opal pulled the collar of her jacket up and took her first step toward the heart of the protest that was forming. The Washington Mall was alive with sound as Opal joined the stream of protesters winding their way toward the steps of the Lincoln Memorial. From all corners of the country, hundreds of thousands of people were beginning to gather. The air buzzed with an urgency she hadn't expected. Every face she passed had a story and reason for being there. Some carried signs while others wore shirts emblazoned with slogans like "Stop the War" or "Peace Now." Opal had not made a sign; she was there to stand witness, to let her body speak where her voice hadn't found the courage to do so yet.

Despite the crowd, Opal felt strangely alone. It wasn't the loneliness of isolation, but the kind of solitude that came from stepping into a world of struggle and protest she hadn't thought to question before. She paused, glancing around at the sea of people before her. Something inside her stirred. She was in awe of the people around her. There were so many people here: mothers, fathers, soldiers, and students, a mixture of ages and status. Their faces spoke of the same thing: a deep, aching need for change.

A woman with long flowing hair and a guitar strung across her back approached her, grinning as she stopped in front of her. "First time?" she asked, her eyes bright with the fervor of youth. Opal nodded, swallowing the nervousness in her throat.

"Well, welcome," she said, offering her a peace sign with her fingers. "You've picked a hell of a day. They're expecting something big, you know. They're going to hear us today. They won't be able to ignore us anymore."

Opal managed a small smile and returned the peace sign awkwardly. "I reckon that's the plan," she breathed.

As the woman walked off, strumming a few chords on her guitar, Opal turned back to the crowd, her heart pounding in her chest. She had made the right decision to come. She couldn't put it into words, but standing there in the middle of so many people who shared a common cause, it felt like something was waking inside her. She walked on, following the flow of the crowd, as the voices of speakers in the distance grew louder. In front of the Lincoln Memorial, a stage had been set up, and a group of people were preparing to speak. Opal took a seat on the steps, leaning against the cold stone, and watched as the first speaker took the microphone. The speaker, a woman in her twenties with dark eyes and a determined look on her face, spoke with passion, urging the crowd to keep fighting for peace. She didn't speak in abstract terms about policy or politics; she spoke about real things like children losing their fathers, about mothers who cried every night, and soldiers who came home broken. The crowd cheered loudly for her.

Opal felt the stirrings of something she couldn't name; a fierce yearning to not just listen, but to act. The woman's words were a direct challenge to everything Opal had known about the world. She was never afraid to be herself in a world that demanded conformity. Everyone knew that Opal Tyler was spontaneous and in a class all her own. She was never afraid of being labeled too much or odd. She welcomed those labels if anyone dared to speak them aloud, but there was something mighty different about stepping outside the neat boundaries she had created for herself in Rhinestone. But the war, Vietnam, and everything that came with it, was bigger than her fears.

As the speeches continued, Opal's eyes scanned the crowd once more, and her mind wandered back to Rhinestone. Rhinestone had always been a quiet town where things moved slowly, where people knew everyone's business, and where the biggest excitement was the annual county fair nearby in Junction. But even in Rhinestone, the war had touched everyone. When the draft cards had arrived in the mailboxes of her neighbors, she had seen the fear in the eyes of mothers whose sons were too young to be sent off. She had heard the whispers of how the local boys, her own friends, were being sent off to fight. Some never came back. And that was what had pushed her to this place. It wasn't about protesting for the sake of protesting. It wasn't about some idealized version of what the world could be. It was about real people and real lives being lost.

When the next speaker, a slim, shaggy-haired man with glasses, took the mic, Opal noticed that the crowd grew more subdued. He spoke of the sacrifices of those who had served in Vietnam, and how they had returned home to be treated like criminals. Opal shifted uncomfortably. Her thoughts returned to the young men in her town, the ones who had gone to Vietnam, their bodies either buried in the red earth of a foreign land or left broken and empty in a hospital bed at home. She thought of Thomas and her friends who liked to dance to old sad songs at the VA some evenings. She knew that some of them would be here today in the crowd.

The speaker's voice rose with emotion, but Opal's attention drifted, her gaze shifting once more to the crowd. She shifted uncomfortably on the stone steps of the Lincoln Memorial. The voices around her shouted in unison, fueled by the low hum of helicopters above. The temperature was still cool, but the heat of the day was already starting to press in, making her feel even more self-conscious in her long-sleeve blouse. She hadn't told anyone she was coming. Not her friends back home in Rhinestone; not even Ms. Belva. Opal didn't think they'd disapprove of the protest itself; after all, everyone was talking about it back home. Even old Eugene Miller, the retired school principal, had made his opinions known when he'd loudly declared at a townhall that he "he wasn't for letting the government think they could control the people." Opal hadn't been worried about them condemning her actions. What she feared, what made her heart ache as she walked out the door of her small house with a suitcase packed for the Greyhound, was the worry she would cause. The long nights of pacing, the phone calls to check in, the concern about her safety. That was what had kept her quiet. She wasn't a young girl anymore. She knew what people would think if she told them. They'd say, "Opal, you're just one person, and look how big this protest is. Don't get yourself mixed up in that mess." She knew, too, that a protest in D.C. wasn't just marching and chanting. There were rumors of violence, whispers about clashes between protesters and the National Guard. And while she wasn't naïve enough to think things would remain peaceful, she didn't want her friends and neighbors to worry. They already had enough on their plates. They all knew someone who had a son or nephew fighting in the war. If they knew Opal had decided to march right into the heart of the chaos, they'd be upset.

For a moment, Opal allowed herself to imagine the scene back in Rhinestone, back home in the small beauty salon. Ms. Belva would've shaken her head, sighing and muttering, "Opal, you're too good-hearted for this kind of thing. What if something happens?" It was exactly the kind of thing Opal had wanted to avoid. But she also knew that Ms. Belva would have given her some rolled up cash and told her to call her if anything got out of hand. Ms. Belva was a force to be reckoned with on her own.

The sound of the crowd chanting began to swell again. The speaker at the podium was saying something about the government's lies and about the people's right to resist. Opal inhaled sharply as a helicopter passed overhead. The crowd around her had begun to grow more restless. She noticed a group of men on the far side of the steps wearing dark clothing and carrying flags with a clenched fist emblazoned on them. They were young, their faces fierce and determined. And yet, something about their presence made Opal uneasy. They weren't just protesting; they were calling for something more, something more obvious. She heard them shouting, urging the crowd to take more aggressive action to disrupt the very fabric of government itself. A group of women nearby were holding hands, their arms raised in a show of solidarity. Opal tried to focus on them, trying to push back the unease in her stomach. But as the sounds of clashing voices and growing agitation in the crowd began to rise, she could feel the tension in the air. The protest was no longer just a statement of peaceful dissent; it was becoming a battle.

In that moment, Opal realized the magnitude of what she had joined. This wasn't Rhinestone. This wasn't the small world she'd known her whole life. Washington, D.C., was a powder keg, and she was standing right in the middle of it. She thought about the bus ride up here. It had been quiet, almost meditative, as the miles passed, each one carrying her farther from the world she knew. When they stopped for lunch, she had thought about calling her friends to let them know she was safe, but something stopped her. The idea of hearing their voices, their concern, their hesitation had felt like an anchor, so she'd kept her silence. She hadn't wanted them to know. But here, in the thick of the protest, the gravity of her decision settled more heavily on her shoulders. She wanted to be part of something bigger, but could she handle the consequences? Could she deal with the fallout if things went sideways? She had never been a fighter. That was always Maude's area of expertise. Between the three of them, Maude was the only one who had ever gotten to tiffs with people. One time in grade school, she punched the older seventh grade bully in the nose when he picked on her brother. But this war was too much. And now, here she was, surrounded by thousands of people demanding an end to it, demanding justice for the lives lost. Opal had come this far, and something in her heart told her that backing away now would feel like defeat.

The sun was dipping lower in the sky when the first clash came. It started as an argument between two groups: one chanting for peace, the other shouting about revolution and change. Opal was far enough away that she couldn't make out the words, but she could feel the rising tension in the air. Her pulse quickened. The crowd began to murmur, and Opal could feel her heart race. The woman with the guitar who had welcomed her to the protest earlier suddenly dropped her instrument and stood frozen. She wasn't smiling anymore. Her face had gone pale, her body tense. Opal's mind raced. Was it really happening? Was this it? The reason she'd kept her distance from her friends, the reason she hadn't told anyone she was coming?

Her hands shook as she gripped her purse. The words about standing up and challenging authority flashed through her mind. Was she strong enough? Could she stand up to the fear, to the possibility that this protest could become something much darker? Then she looked around and remembered that she wasn't alone. These strangers were all here for the same reason. They weren't backing down. They were standing for what they believed in, no matter the cost. Opal stood up, her body moving almost automatically, as the sounds of confrontation grew closer. She wasn't sure what she would do, what part she would play in all of this. But at least she had come. At least she had shown up. For the first time in a long time, she felt the rush of something inside that rivaled determination.

Chapter Twelve

The sound of marching boots grew louder, and Opal's breath caught in her throat. The National Guard was making its way through the crowd now, their heavy boots striking the concrete like a drumbeat signaling the start of something far more serious than she had imagined. The murmur in the crowd shifted, turning to whispers of concern, but no one was moving. No one was backing down. Opal's gaze darted across the protestors all around her. Some people were sitting down on the grass with their hands raised in peace signs, while others stood rigid with their eyes locked on the advancing soldiers. The faces around her were a mixture of fear, resolve, and anger. She felt all of it swirl inside her like a storm waiting to break. A voice suddenly broke through the tension, cutting sharply through the air. "Stand your ground! Don't back down!" A young woman near Opal shouted it, her eyes wild, her fists clenched at her sides.

Opal's pulse quickened as she instinctively took a step back, her heart hammering. She had known this could get tense. She had heard the rumors about the clashes from earlier protests. But now, standing in the center of it, she could feel the electricity in the air—an overwhelming tension that seemed to pulse through her bones. What the hell had she gotten herself into? A tall man with a red bandana was yelling something about non-violent resistance, but there was something in his voice that sounded more like a warning than a call to action. People weren't backing away; they were stepping forward. The protestors closest to the National Guard locked eyes with the soldiers. There was no fear in their expressions, just quiet resolve. Some of them began chanting again, louder now, their voices blending into a single, unified sound: "Hell no, we won't go!"

It wasn't just a chant anymore; it was a declaration. The movement had become a defiant, unyielding statement that couldn't be ignored. She took a deep breath and looked around. The entire scene felt surreal. People of all ages were standing shoulder to shoulder, facing down the line of soldiers, unarmed but unafraid. Her heart swelled with pride. She didn't know how to explain it, but she knew that today would matter. There was no turning back now. She had come this far, and she couldn't just walk away, couldn't just slip back into the quiet life she had left behind in Rhinestone. This was it. This was her moment.

The soldiers were closer now, their helmets gleaming in the waning sunlight. Opal could see the faint shimmer of their shields, and the cold, hardened expressions on their faces. Some were even whispering among themselves, while others stood stiff and silent, their eyes scanning the crowd. There was a palpable sense of unease in the air, like the whole situation was teetering on the edge of something dangerous. She swallowed hard, the lump in her throat making it hard to breathe.

"Hey, come on, let's go!" A voice suddenly broke through the tension beside her. It was a man, his hand on her arm, his grip firm but not unkind. Opal turned quickly, her heart jumping in her chest. It was Sam, a wounded veteran from her hometown. "What are you doing?" he asked, his eyes wide with concern. He was looking at the National Guard, then back at her, his expression torn. "This is getting out of hand. We need to go."

Opal's pulse was still racing. She felt dizzy, unsure of what to do, but something inside her, the same part that had dragged her here in the first place, pushed her to stay. "No," she said, shaking her head as she pulled her arm gently from his grasp. "I can't leave now. I need to be here, Sam. I need to be part of this." Her voice shook, but there was a quiet determination in it that surprised even her.

Sam sighed, running his hand through his messy hair. "You're not scared?" he asked, his voice gentle but tinged with worry. Opal nodded slowly. "I am. I don't know what's going to happen, but I can't go back now. I have to do something."

Sam stood silently for a moment, looking at her, the conflict on his face clear. "I get it. But Opal, this is bigger than us. People are getting hurt at these things. I've seen it."

"I'm not afraid of getting hurt," she said, her voice trembling but firm. "I'm afraid of what happens if no one does anything. I have to do this for me and for you and for Theodore and William and Tyler and Lawrence and Phillip and all the others."

Sam's eyes softened, the concern still there but mixed with a deep understanding. He took a step back, his shoulders sagging. "Okay. But promise me you'll be careful. If anything happens to you, all of Rhinestone will revolt."

"I will," Opal cut in, placing a hand on his arm. "I'm not going to do anything stupid. I just, I have to stand here. I have to show them that we're not going to take it anymore. I have to show them that there's nothing left to give them."

The sound of a megaphone cracked through the air, and the voice on the loudspeaker was clear, calm, and somehow commanding. "We are here for peace," it said. "We are here for justice. We are here for the lives of the soldiers, the families, the children. Do not let them send us back to war. Stand strong." The crowd roared in response, their voices rising into a unified wave of anger and hope. Opal felt the words in her chest, in her bones. She found herself shouting along with them, her voice rising in defiance.

"Hell no, we won't go!"

The chant felt good. It felt righteous. It was like a weight had lifted from her chest. The tension between the protesters and the National Guard was palpable. Everyone seemed to be holding their breath. And then, just as quickly as it had started, the sound of a loud explosion rang out across the Mall, followed by the screech of sirens in the distance. A few people screamed, and Opal felt a rush of panic flood through her veins. Her heart thudded, her hands shook. Was this it? Was this where it all fell apart?

The crowd, still chanting, didn't break. They didn't scatter. They held their ground, their voices louder now. And somehow, despite the fear, despite the chaos in the air, Opal found herself standing taller and stronger. She was a part of something bigger.

Another voice from the front of the crowd shouted, "Don't let them silence you! Hell no, we won't go!"

Opal's heart pounded in her chest, the echo of the chant still reverberating in her mind. "Hell no, we won't go!" She wasn't sure if the words were a promise, a defiance, or just a way to fill the silence between the fear and the chaos that was suddenly bubbling all around her. The explosion that had come from somewhere beyond the steps of the Capitol had sent a wave of panic through the crowd. But even in the midst of the chaos, Opal noticed that most people didn't panic. They didn't run. Instead, they moved together, closer to the steps, as though creating an unspoken barricade between themselves and the soldiers. She hadn't thought this would happen. She hadn't thought it would escalate this quickly. When she'd boarded the round trip Greyhound bus to Washington, she'd expected a march, a crowd of people, a bit of noise. But this was something different. The tension in the air felt like static, the kind that came just before a storm broke. Sam had slipped away in the confusion, no doubt to get to safer ground. Opal didn't blame him. His fear had been real and his hesitation understandable. He probably felt like he was back in the active war zone that had almost taken his life. Maybe she should have gone with him, but Opal was doing something that she needed to do for herself. She had come here for a reason, to stand for something larger than herself, and she wasn't about to let fear send her back to the quiet life she had left behind. She wasn't going to let anything take away this moment.

But even as she told herself that, she knew it wasn't as simple as just standing here. The guards were closing in, their boots louder now, their faces unreadable behind their shields. The chants were louder too, the crowd almost deafening as they pressed forward, a mass of human bodies pushing toward the front. Opal's hands clenched at her sides. The sound of helicopters buzzing overhead only added to the sense of urgency. She could feel the heat rising from the concrete beneath her feet, the smell of sweat and smoke thick in the air. She had to keep her head, she had to stay calm. Her thoughts drifted, as they so often did when she felt overwhelmed back to Rhinestone. Back to the small town where people didn't make waves, where life was predictable, and where the biggest danger was a stray dog running through the streets or a broken light bulb at the church. Rhinestone wasn't Washington, D.C. It wasn't a place where you had to stand in the middle of a protest, shoulder to shoulder with strangers, with the full knowledge that things could turn ugly. Rhinestone didn't know this kind of chaos. Rhinestone didn't know the weight of the world hanging in the balance. And yet, despite the fear creeping up in her throat, Opal found herself filled with an overwhelming sense of pride. She was here. She was making a stand. Her fingers brushed the embroidered peace symbol on her purse again, a small, steadying reminder of why she had come.

By the time the sun had fully set, the National Guard had made their presence known in full force. The first wave of protestors had begun to move away from the steps of the Capitol, but not because they wanted to leave. It was a tactical retreat, a way to reassemble, to regroup in the face of the threat of violence. But Opal wasn't ready to move. She had come for this, and no matter how uncomfortable it felt, she needed to be here. The day's protest had shifted, and now, at the cusp of night, it was beginning to take on an entirely different tone. The National Guard was on alert, their movements stiffer, their weapons more visible.

Opal felt her resolve falter slightly as the first tear gas canisters began to fall into the crowd. There was a brief, painful pause, then, a panic surged through the people closest to the front. The crowd surged backward, people shouting, hands pressed to their faces as they tried to shield themselves from the fumes. Her eyes watered as she wiped them with the back of her hand, her throat burning from the smoke. It was hard to breathe, hard to focus on anything except the stinging in her lungs. She pressed her palms to the stone of the Capitol steps, steadying herself as the crowd began to move again. But the truth was undeniable now: this wasn't just a protest. She was in danger. For the first time since she'd arrived, Opal considered leaving. She thought of the return bus ticket in her pocket, the one that would take her back to Rhinestone.

People were beginning to set up tents and sleeping bags wherever they could. Benches and monuments held small groups of people who sought shelter for the night. She was caught in the thick of it, uncertain about her place in this sea of shouting voices. The rally had taken on a wild rhythm now, the music from earlier replaced by drums and chanting that seemed to roll through the crowd like thunder. If she left now, would she regret it? Could she live with herself if she didn't fight for peace? As the night wore on, she felt the weight of her decision like a stone lodged deep in her chest. Every part of her wanted to just leave, to head back to the Greyhound station and get on the bus back to Rhinestone. She could walk inside her front door and no one would ever know where she had been. But she knew she couldn't leave. Not yet. Not after everything she had seen. She had one more night in Washington. One more night to be part of this rebellion, to feel what it was like to stand for something. She wasn't sure what it would mean for her, but she knew it was something she had to do. She had no idea if she would be able to leave the protest peacefully, or if she would be forced to leave in a hurry. But she would not back down.

Somewhere in the noise Opal dozed off to sleep with her back against a bench. The following morning she woke to the sound of the morning news crackling through a nearby radio. Her heart sank as she listened to the reports of what had transpired the night before. Tear gas had been used, arrests made, and the streets of Washington had erupted into pocketed groups of chaos. She decided to walk for a bit to clear her mind and hopefully find a strong cup of coffee. She needed a shower. She needed some hot soup. She needed her bed where she could wrap up in a blanket and sleep off the exhaustion. She needed a pen and some paper so she could write down everything she was feeling, even though she knew she would never forget this quick trip to Washington or Atlas or the woman with the guitar.

She was grateful that she had been safe and could step back on the bus to head home. She was thankful to have seen what she saw, to have heard what she heard, to have smelled what she smelled. She felt both heavy and light, sad and determined. The journey back to Rhinestone was a quiet one, but as she sat in the bus, surrounded by strangers, she could feel the weight of her decisions settling on her. The protest, the people, and chants felt like a dream now. The bus hit a pothole, jolting her from her reverie. Her reflection in the window was a woman she hadn't known she could be; a woman who had stood at the edge of something dangerous and felt the pull of revolution. And now, the road was taking her home to continue her mission however she could.

Chapter Thirteen

Opal was back in the salon that next Tuesday afternoon much to everyone's glee. Ms. Belva smiled at her when she walked in the door ready to tackle their long list of clients. She knew that Opal had not been at a conference, but she also could tell that Opal didn't want to talk about where she had been, so she didn't push it.

Opal had never lied to her friends and family members, but when asked how the conference was, Opal merely shrugged and said it was indeed life changing, before changing the subject to what she was planning on cooking for dinner that evening. Maude and Ruby both sensed that there was something that Opal was going through, something she wasn't quite ready to talk about just yet, but they didn't push. Though every night when the news station played videos and flashed pictures across the screen, Ruby searched every face on the screen for her friend. One day Opal would feel comfortable telling her two most trusted friends about her weekend away, and they would be there for her when she did.

It was a warm spring evening when Jameson sat down with his young daughter in the living room after a long day at the office. Ruby was drying the dishes she had just washed after supper and the television flickered, showing images of chaos as police, soldiers, and students clashed in Washington, D.C. that evening. As they watched, Ruby walked quietly into the room and sighed. She had always wanted to protect her daughter's innocence as the terrible tragedies creeped closer to their perfect world in Rhinestone. She could see the confusion in Melanie's eyes, the innocence still clinging to her view of the world.

"Why are they fighting, Daddy?" Melanie asked quietly, her small voice full of concern.

Jameson paused for a moment, unsure of how to explain the complexities of what was unfolding on the screen, and what had unfolded across the country in the past few years. He realized that maybe now, of all times, it was important to talk to her about history; the kind of history they were both living through. He settled into the worn armchair and began to tell her the story of the May Day protests in Washington, D.C. that were being replayed on the screen in front of them. He took off his glasses and cleaned them with the simple white handkerchief from his pocket.

"You see, Melanie, a lot of what you're seeing on the television right now is a result of something very complicated, something that has been building for many years. It's about a war, one that our country got involved in, far from home, in a place called Vietnam. Now, I know you're too young to understand all of the details, but let me tell you what I know about it, and maybe, just maybe, it'll help you understand why people are so upset and why people are in the streets fighting," he said calmly.

Ruby sat down on the couch next to the lamp on the end table and picked up the book she had abandoned a few days before, but Jameson knew that she was listening as intently as their daughter was. The Vietnam War had been going on for a long time by 1971, for more than a decade. It had begun as a conflict between North Vietnam, led by the communist government of Ho Chi Minh, and South Vietnam, backed by the United States. It was a war that he and Ruby were deeply familiar with, as they had both lost cousins to the jungle warfare. "At first, we sent a few advisors to help the South Vietnamese, but over time, our involvement deepened. By the time the 1960s rolled around, American troops were fully engaged in a brutal and bloody war. The reasons for our involvement were tangled in the Cold War—the fear that if Vietnam fell to communism, other countries in Southeast Asia would follow. The government told us it was a fight against the spread of communism, a fight to protect freedom and democracy," Jameson continued. He wasn't sure how much Melanie had learned in school or if the young girl even knew what communism was, but she didn't interrupt to ask questions.

"Over the years, as the fighting escalated, more and more people began to question whether we were really doing the right thing. Young people, college students, mostly, became some of the strongest voices in opposition. They didn't want to fight a war in a foreign land that seemed so far removed from their own struggles. The death tolls mounted, and the media brought the horrors of the war into living rooms across America. The war's brutality was no longer something abstract, something that could be ignored. It was real, and it was happening to real people," Jameson explained.

"Are we doing the right thing?" Melanie breathed. "Why can't people just be nice to each other?"

"I don't know," Jameson winced. This was the first war that anyone had ever seen play out live on the television screen. The American Revolution and the Civil War were seen in portraits painted on the battlefield. World War I and World War II sent back blurry photographs and grainy videos that didn't fully show the horrors of what those men and women experienced.

"So, what's happening, Melanie, was a culmination of all that anger and frustration. People are tired of the war, tired of the lies they feel they're being told by their government, tired of watching their friends and brothers come home in body bags. Thousands of young people gather all over the country to protest, to demand that the war end. So far it's been one of the biggest movements we have ever seen, and it was aimed directly at the very heart of our government," Jameson detailed.

"And that's far away from here?" Melanie asked.

"It's not close to us, no," Jameson answered.

"Is this what y'all watch on television every day?" Melanie asked. She had inched closer to Jameson on the floor and looked up at him.

Jameson nodded. "I was sitting in my office when I first heard about the protests." As a lawyer in the South, Jameson's life was rooted in tradition, in order, in stability, but even he couldn't ignore the growing unrest. "We have had our own protests down here, of course, though they were often about civil rights, about the fight for equality and justice in a country that still hasn't fully embraced those principles. But this, this is different. The protests in Washington were about something bigger, about the soul of the nation itself. The war, the government, the military-industrial complex, it is all under fire. I watched as the television showed hundreds of young people, students, hippies, activists, marching through the streets of Washington. Some of them were ready to face arrest, even violence, if that's what it took to make their voices heard."

"Did people die?" Melanie gulped.

"I don't think so," Jameson said. "At least not at this one particular protest."

"Thousands of people have been killed so far though," Ruby whispered. "The war has taken so many."

"And that's why these people want to protest? Are they wrong for wanting to fight back?" Melanie asked. Jameson could see that she was trying to understand and process everything that she was hearing.

"Melly, I want you to understand that these

young people are not bad people. They aren't all criminals or troublemakers, as some people say. They're scared just like everyone else. They are also very angry, just like everyone else. Some of them had brothers or fathers who were fighting in Vietnam, and they didn't want to see them sent over there to die. Others were just tired of watching innocent people, both Americans and Vietnamese, lose their lives in a war that seems endless," Jameson said gently.

The protests were a dramatic expression of frustration. The May Day protests were meant to shut down the government. The protesters blocked streets, held sit-ins, and staged marches that were intended to cripple the city. The numbers were staggering—thousands of demonstrators, many of them young, some of them just teenagers, all of them united by the belief that they had to do something, anything, to stop the war. And the government responded with overwhelming force. The National Guard was called in, and soon, streets that had once been peaceful became battlegrounds. "I thought that that protest could be the turning point, the moment when the country finally realizes the war has to end," Ruby whispered. She loved her country and was a proud supporter of the military, but she couldn't pretend that she was not confused and angry and utterly devastated at watching the news every evening.

"A lot of people thought that," Opal said suddenly. No one had heard her come inside the house.

"Oh, Opal! You scared me to death," Ruby

gasped. "You have a bad habit of doing this kind of thing!"

"Sorry, Rubes! I was just returning your pie plate from the other day. I knocked a few times but no one came to the door. I had to make sure you weren't in any danger or anything. Plus, the door was unlocked," she smirked.

Jameson chuckled and said, "Speaking of pie, there's a few slices of chocolate pie in the fridge with my name on it. Y'all want a slice while I'm up?"

Ruby, Opal, and Melanie all shook their heads. Jameson shrugged and skipped off to the kitchen to satisfy his sweet tooth. Opal sat down next to Melanie on the floor and continued in Jameson's absence. "It wasn't just students, Melly. It was also a lot of ordinary folks. People who had been sent to fight in Vietnam and came back broken, mentally and physically scarred. Some of them couldn't live with what they'd seen or with what they'd done. Others returned to find that no one cared that they were treated as if they were the enemy. And that made people angry, too. The government had sent them to fight for something they didn't understand, and now they were left to pick up the pieces of their broken lives. Many of these people, veterans, I mean, joined the protests, too, because they wanted the war to stop, and they wanted the country to finally face what had happened."

As they watched the scenes replay on the television screen, they couldn't help but feel a deep sense of unease. The images of protestors being dragged away, of police wielding their nightsticks, of the burning fires in the streets—it was all too much. The people on the streets weren't just rebelling for the sake of rebellion, they believed they were fighting for their lives, for their futures, and for the right to live in a country that didn't send its young men and women to die in senseless wars. "Here in the South, the protests and riots feel different. The South has always been a place of traditions and hierarchies, where politics were heavily influenced by old ways of thinking, and it has sometimes felt like we were separate from the rest of the country. We have our own drama, of course, but this feels different. The war in Vietnam has changed all that. It pulled everyone into the same boiling pot of frustration and anger. Whether you were from the North or the South, whether you were a liberal or a conservative, whether you were a student or a lawyer like your daddy— it didn't matter. The war had a way of uniting everyone under its cloud of grief," Opal continued. "Not everyone agreed with the protesters. There are plenty of people who still believe the war was a fight worth fighting. They think America had a duty to stop the spread of communism, and they didn't trust anyone who protests, whom they say are disrupting the peace and disrespecting the very country that gave them freedom. And I can understand that, to an extent, but what I don't understand is why the government doesn't listen. Why do they keep sending young men to die? Why don't they understand that this senseless killing has to stop?"

"It makes me sad," Melanie said. Her eyes were

glued to the television, but Ruby quickly stood up and turned off the screen. "I think it's time for bed, Melly," she whispered softly. To her surprise, Melanie did not object. She waved goodbye to Opal as Ruby promised to be upstairs in a few minutes to tuck her in.

"It makes me sad, too," Ruby admitted to Opal. She rubbed her friend's arm and saw the sadness in her eyes. She knew that Opal had seen the hardships of war more than she had with her friendships down at the VA Center. She thought back to the long debates at the dinner table she had heard friends talk about, the arguments between family and friends, the way the news was filled with angry voices, each side convinced the other was wrong. It was clear that the nation was divided. Even within her own circles—among the lawyers and businessmen that Jameson spent most of his time with, even the professors and soldiers, there were deep divides over the war. Some of them were adamant that the protests were nothing more than anarchy, that the demonstrators were unpatriotic and misguided. Others, though, understood the deeper truths that lay beneath the surface in the ways in which this war had taken a terrible toll on the nation's conscience.

"I wish we could all hide our children from the sadness of the world. Remember what the Irish poet, William Butler Yeats, once wrote? 'A terrible beauty is born.' Oh, Opal, he was talking about things such as this. It's so hard being a mother. I can't imagine having a son and sending him off to war. How do you explain that to anyone," Ruby lamented.

"It's hard to explain to anyone," Opal sighed. "Maybe one day, when we're older, we will understand better. We're literally witnessing history, Ruby. And I can't escape the feeling that we aren't done being witnesses either."

"I think you're right, Opal. I think you're going to live a very long time and you're going to bear witness to all sorts of history. In fact, I think you're going to change the world," Ruby smiled. She hugged Opal as they walked to the front door.

"Maybe so," Opal smiled softly. "Maybe so."

"Do you want to talk about it yet?" Ruby asked gently.

Opal looked up at Ruby and shook her head. "No, not quite yet."

Chapter Fourteen

Melanie had long dozed off in the fourth pew from the front early one Sunday morning. Maude couldn't blame her; she was seconds away from closing her eyes and ignoring the incessant rambling of Nadine Waters who stood with the preacher at the front of the church at the spot where the carpet was the most frayed. New carpet for the church was probably on their list of things to replace as well. This was a faded shade of what was once a vibrant red, but the years and foot traffic had tarnished the threads tremendously. Nadine had already been rambling for twenty minutes and there was no end in sight. People shifted uncomfortably in their seats as a baby whined loudly near the back pew. At least the baby had an excuse to whine about the scene in front of them. It would be unbecoming for Maude to wail out loud.

"Thank you, Sister Waters," the preacher nodded again. It was hard for him to get a word in edgewise. As soon as Nadine took a deep breath, he saw his opportunity. He shook her hand vigorously and waved his hand over her as to anoint her. "Beaver Crossing Holy Church for the Faithful is incredibly blessed to have you and the Ladies Auxiliary as a part of our congregation. Thanks to you the roof repairs will begin this coming Tuesday and Lloyd Weathers has assured me that the baptismal will be completed by the end of next month. We are so blessed that you gave your time and talents to this sacred, holy place."

The rest of the congregation began to clap as Margaret began to play the organ. Nadine took her seat on the front row in between Lulu and Patsy who were seated along the front row with the rest of the Auxiliary members. They all had smiles plastered on their faces, but even they had begun to fidget in their seats at Nadine's longwindedness.

When the service ended a few minutes later, Maude had to once again wait while members of the church again congratulated Nadine and the rest of the ladies. She was never going to get her favorite seat at the all-you-could eat buffet at this rate. The coveted table closest to the dessert area was never empty for long. She thought about waking Melanie and the two of them hightailing it across town, but the restaurant had a policy of not seating anyone until their entire party was present. Ruby and Opal were surrounded by people and Maude couldn't even make eye contact with them. She wasn't sure what all anyone had left to talk about; they had all been talking about this long enough. The ladies were already planning their next outreach mission; they had settled on a bake-sale down at the school to raise money for something or another at the school. Maude had not been listening, even though bake sales ranked much higher on her list than a telethon had. As annoying as some of these women in the town were, they were all mostly excellent cooks and Maude had a sweet tooth that could never be fully satiated.

After what felt like forever, the group of people disbanded and everyone walked outside to their respective vehicles. "Y'all about ready?" Jameson called over his shoulder.

"Yes!" Maude said. She slammed the door to her car and peeled out of the grassy makeshift parking spot before anyone could respond. She was bound and determined to get her favorite table. Betsy's homemade cakes and pies were legendary, and Maude set out to taste whatever it was that Betsy had set her mind to baking that day. She hoped that Betsy had made another one of her famous layered chocolate cakes. She wasn't sure what it was technically called since every cookbook called for a different number of layers. Some made twelve, some made thirteen, and some made seventy-five. There was no wrong answer when it came to chocolate cake.

Maude pulled into the first parking spot she saw in the bustling parking lot a few minutes later. When you didn't abide by normal traffic laws or follow the speed limit, you tend to arrive much quicker than those who follow the rules. Maude walked to the front door and stood by the doorway and tapped her foot impatiently. Where were they? Why were they taking so long! Opal had probably stopped to dawdle along the way, but Jameson and Ruby knew the importance of eating on time and getting the perfect table.

When Jameson and Ruby finally pulled into the parking lot, Maude ripped open the door and quickly marched to the hostess station. "Five people," she all but barked.

"Ms. Cooper, always a pleasure," the woman behind the counter smiled wryly. "Is the rest of your party here?"

"Yes, they're walking in now," Maude grimaced. Thankfully, Jameson held the door open and ushered Ruby and Melanie inside. "I only see four," the woman mumbled.

"Opal runs on her own time," Maude scowled. She should have snatched her up and tossed her into the car before leaving the church, but it was too late to think on that. She peered over the hostess stand to see what the availability was. A nicely dressed family was sitting at her table and they looked to have just arrived. Maude frowned and slumped her shoulders. The closest open table was a good twenty feet away from the dessert line.

"This way," the woman said. She decided to bend the rules on waiting for the rest of the party because Maude Cooper was known to get a little touchy when it came to food. "Opal should be here any minute," Ruby explained timidly. "She was right behind us."

"Oh, I love Opal," the woman replied. "She is just the sweetest! As soon as she comes in I'll bring her over."

"Everyone knows Opal," Maude replied. How in the world this tiny little woman could flit around all the time boggled her mind. She had never known Opal to ever tire of anything or anyone. Opal never met a stranger; she always said there was no such thing as strangers because everyone was connected or some mumbo jumbo. Opal was the only person she knew that was beloved by everyone. If she ever met someone who didn't care for Opal, she'd use that as a measuring stick for their character. Though Opal often aggravated her, there was no better person in the world than Opal Clementine Tyler.

Anytime the front door to the restaurant opened, Maude looked up and then scowled when it wasn't Opal. "She was right behind you?" she asked Ruby for the fifth time.

"Oh, just go ahead and start without her," Ruby sighed. It was true that Opal had been parked behind them, but whether or not she left the parking lot was another question entirely. Opal bounced along to the beat of her own drum. One time she had followed a butterfly down a country lane for a mile or so just because.

Maude didn't need to be told twice. She walked over to the buffet line and grabbed a warm plate. She piled it high with fried chicken, mashed potatoes and gravy, and two rolls. Betsy's homemade pot roast wafted over the counter, which warranted another plate. She set the first plate down on the table and walked right back up to the line with her second plate. The pot roast smelled delicious. She made sure not to get too many carrots because they were not her favorite. Before she walked away, a man behind the counter set out a new pan of dumplings which she couldn't say no to. That left just enough room for green beans. She wasn't an avid fan of vegetables, but the green beans cooked in bacon fat was another story. It was healthy and delicious at the same time.

"Did you save any for the rest of us?" Ruby quipped as Maude sat down next to her.

"She still ain't here?" Maude ignored Ruby looking around for Opal.

"No," Ruby frowned. "I guess we better go ahead, too."

Melanie dutifully followed her mother and father to fix her plate. She too had her eye on the thick slices of chocolate cake that Mrs. Betsy was famous for, but she knew her mother would never allow her to skip straight to dessert. Her mother played by the rules, so Melanie allowed her mother to scoop mashed potatoes, macaroni and cheese, green beans, fried chicken, and rice onto her plate. Melanie loved to eat, but she had a sweet tooth that more closely resembled Maude's. Though her father, Jameson, was known to sneak ice cream any chance he got, and Melanie knew exactly when to meet him downstairs in the kitchen for a bowl of homemade vanilla ice cream with chocolate fudge sauce over the top. Sometimes Jameson threw a few slices of banana into the bowl to make it healthier, which always made Ruby giggle.

Maude was already halfway through her second plate of food by the time Opal made it over to their table. "Where have you been?" Maude asked her.

"Well, I've been all over yet nowhere at all when I really think about it," Opal mused.

"I meant where have you been since church! I swear, Opal, one of these days!" Maude began, but Opal had already walked over to the salad bar to begin filling her plate with all things green. Maude grimaced at the sight of Opal's plate that looked like it came straight out of a health and wellness magazine. Opal had been a vegetarian for years and though she never pushed that lifestyle on her friends, it made Maude gag at the thought of only eating what she referred to as rabbit food.

"I just love how crisp the lettuce is. And these carrots are perfect," Opal said. She looked over at the last few bites of food on Maude's plate and grinned. "Would you like some of my salad?"

"Negative," Maude said. She was toying between getting a few more bites of that delectable pot roast, but the slices of cake were dwindling on the dessert counter, so she made a beeline towards the counter lined with cakes, pies, and various desserts in pans. She helped herself to a slice of cake, a scoop of banana pudding, and a healthy helping of peach cobbler. As soon as she sat down, Melanie's eyes widened at the size of the slice of cake on Maude's place. "That looks good," the young girl smiled.

"As soon as you finish up on those vegetables you can have a slice," Ruby reminded her.

"Yes ma'am," Melanie nodded. She quickly ate what was left on her plate and followed Ruby to the dessert line where she got one of the last few slices of the layered cake that dripped with chocolate icing. Ruby decided that a scoop of banana pudding would suit her best, but Jameson joined Maude and Melanie by choosing the thick slice of cake.

As soon as Melanie, Ruby, Jameson, and Maude were finished with their desserts, they waited for Opal to finish her meal. Opal was the slowest eater they knew, as she liked to savor every bite. Once she was finished with her salad, she perused the dessert counter and chose the smallest slice of key lime pie. Once she was finished with that, they all wandered outside to the parking lot to their cars. "I've got a couple of branches on the back twenty that I need to cut down. That storm last week near about split the tree in half," Jameson explained.

"Need any help with that?" Opal asked.

"I think I can manage, but if there's anything you need from over yonder, just go ahead and get it," he replied. He was referring to the herbs, flowers, and plants that Opal liked to collect from the forest behind Magnolia Manor. She turned them into tonics and medicinal potions that people from all over flocked to her for.

"I just may take you up on that," Opal smiled. "I was going to volunteer Maude to help hold the ladder if you needed some help. Lord knows we can't give her a saw or anything though."

They all laughed as Jameson started the car and Melanie climbed into the backseat. "Y'all want to come over and go for a walk in the woods while Jameson works?" Ruby asked.

"I've got plenty of buckets and baskets in the car," Opal nodded. "What do you say, Maude?"

"Yea, I can handle that," Maude said.

True to her reputation, Maude beat the others to the Manor. She was sitting on the porch swing by the time Jameson pulled up under the iconic magnolia tree. It was only ten feet tall, but magnolias were known to spread. They hope that one day it would take up much more room. That is, if Maude didn't back over it. She got awfully close more times than Ruby wanted to keep track of. "About time y'all got here!" Maude laughed.

"You ran that red light near Flat Creek!" Ruby shrieked.

"It was orange," Maude shrugged.

"There's no such thing," Ruby rebuffed.

"I told you we need to get her eyes checked," Opal nodded. "Not that it would matter," she added quietly.

"I heard that," Maude grunted.

"Y'all quit squabbling and come on in. I need to change out of these clothes," Ruby said. She headed up the stairs to get out of her church clothes and put on her walking shoes. "Do y'all need to borrow some clothes to go out in the woods?" Ruby asked, but Opal shook her head. "I always keep extra clothes in my car," she smiled proudly. Opal opened the trunk of her small car and pulled out a worn pair of overalls and a pair of boots. "And it looks like Maude is already dressed for the occasion, so we'll just wait on you, Rubes," Opal continued, as she stared at Maude who had worn her comfortable pants and long-sleeved shirt, along with a baseball cap to church and lunch.

Maude made herself at home in the kitchen by pouring herself a glass of sweet tea from Ruby's refrigerator while Ruby was upstairs changing clothes. Melanie bounded down the stairs a few moments later with Jameson at her heels. "I'm going to get a head start out there. Ruby will be down in a minute," Jameson said. Opal exited the downstairs bathroom in her outdoorsy outfit and a straw hat and waited with Maude and Melanie. When Ruby came downstairs a few minutes later, they all walked outside towards the backwoods behind the beautiful home.

Maude pulled out a pack of cigarettes from her purse and lit one up. "I don't know why you still smoke those," Ruby sighed. "They already banned them from the television and radio a few months ago. They aren't good for you, Maude."

"I'm outside," Maude shrugged. "It's healthier out in nature."

"Yea, I don't think that's how that works," Opal said. She led the group down by the creek deep in the holler where she said the best wildflowers grew. She carefully and dutifully selected the best flowers and wild herbs that grew along the muddy bank. "What are you experimenting with this time?" Ruby asked Opal.

"I don't know what to call it just yet, but I'm working with a few things that boost the spirit," Opal said.

"I told you to quit messing with spirits!" Maude hissed. "Unless it's from the liquor cabinet."

"Spirit as in mood. I want to help people be happier, or at least not so sad. I can't explain it,"

Opal sighed. "The men I see down at the center aren't happy. There's no more joy or anything really. They look lost. They feel lost. They're turning to the liquor cabinets as you say, so I want something healthier, more natural. Something that won't make them so lost anymore."

"I think that's a beautiful idea," Ruby smiled.

"I've been working on it with Thomas through our letters. He said the Vietnamese have things like that over there and that it's a good idea. I guess we'll see," Opal said softly. She smelled the wild lavender and wrapped it in a clean handkerchief before putting it in the front pocket of her overalls. "I've got to do something or else I'll lose my mind."

Chapter Fifteen

Ruby sighed quietly and flicked her hair out of her eyes. She had smudges of flour on her nose, cheeks, and the sleeves of her shirt that had been rolled up to her elbows. She was thankful she had thrown on an apron, which was something she normally did not wear when she baked in her kitchen. However, whenever Opal and Maude were around, she knew that an apron would be more than necessary. "Will you two quit it?" she asked for what felt like the tenth time. Out of the corner of her eye she had seen Maude blow a handful of flour onto Opal's back. "I could use some help over here. The bake sale is tomorrow after all."

Maude rolled her eyes at Ruby once again. "Ruby, I am helping with the bake sale. Who do you think buys the cakes and pies? There's only two types of people in this world. Bakers and eaters," Maude explained.

"And Maude is the latter. She definitely does do her part," Opal nodded. She scooped a spoonful of the chocolate chip cookie dough and tasted it. "It needs more vanilla." She opened the bottle of pure vanilla and poured a small amount of the brown liquid in the bowl. Once everything was incorporated, Opal tasted the mixture again and smiled brightly. "Utter perfection."

"Do you ever measure anything?" Maude asked. She already knew the answer to her question before Opal shook her head.

"Some things have to be measured with the heart. Vanilla is one of them," Opal shrugged. "Garlic is another, but I don't suggest putting garlic in a cookie. Unless you have some kind of infection, then maybe substitute the sugar for garlic." She launched into a medical study she had recently read about garlic being a natural remedy for many of life's ailments, but Maude had already felt gagged by the thought of eating a chocolate chip cookie with garlic in it.

"How's that pound cake coming?" Maude asked Ruby.

Ruby looked at the clock above the stove. "It has about eight minutes left," she replied. Maude huffed and walked over to the oven, but Ruby shrieked before she could open the oven door. "Don't you dare open the oven while my pound cake is inside! It'll fall flatter than your hair in a rainstorm if you open the oven door!"

Opal burst out in laughter and slapped her knees. "Ruby's right," she said. "Maude, your hair is flatter than I've ever seen. If you don't stop wearing that dang ball cap, I swear!

"Well, you two are feeling extra rude today," Maude said sulkily. She took the baseball cap off her head and tossed it through the kitchen doorway.

"Are you giving up on the Atlanta Braves already?" Jameson asked. He had Maude's cap in his hands. It had sailed right into his knees as he was walking in through the doorway.

"Never," Maude said. She smiled sheepishly at Jameson who placed the hat on the table. "Boy, it smells good in here!" Jameson chirped. He eyed the mixing bowl full of cookie dough. "Melanie and I are gonna run over to mother and daddy's real quick to help them fix the beam on the porch. Can I get you anything while I'm out?" he asked Ruby.

"I think we are ok here," Ruby smiled. "I've got a few more things to bake before tomorrow's bake sale, but I think we can manage if you don't eat all of our product!" She pushed Jameson's hand away as he sneakily dipped a spoon from the drawer into Opal's chocolate chip cookie dough. "That is good!" he exclaimed. Opal smiled, and then stuck her tongue out at Maude.

"We shouldn't be too long! Oh, I'll bring those pizzas home for supper and see if I can help taste test any more of these delicious treats when we get back," Jameson grinned. Ruby hugged Melanie goodbye and watched out the window as Melanie and Jameson got into Jameson's truck and backed out of the driveway.

"You sure got a good one," Maude nodded. "I thought there was a spell where we were gonna have to shake him up, but it was a brief spell. You've done good."

Ruby smiled and whisked the lemon icing in the metal bowl one more time. She and Jameson had been married for almost eleven years. Their wedding anniversary was in August, but they had been together since they were in high school, which meant that they had been together for half of their lives already. They had broken up one time, right after Ruby had graduated college. Between the pressure of law school and Jameson's family, it had all been too much for them, but fate had a way of making things turn out just how it was supposed to. Melanie was the perfect culmination of their love and there had never been a little girl who was more loved and adored than Melanie Elizabeth Montgomery.

The egg timer went off and Maude jumped up to turn it off. "Don't touch the oven," Ruby reminded her. She turned the oven off and reset the time for five more minutes.

"I thought it was ready?" Maude asked.

"It has to rest in the oven for a little bit," Ruby explained. "I'm keeping an eye on things. Why don't you try this icing and see if it has enough sweetness."

Maude didn't have to be asked twice. She dipped her finger in the bowl of icing and promptly licked the pale yellow icing off her finger. "Delicious," she hummed.

"Maude! Use a spoon!" Ruby hissed. She muttered under breath as she shook her head. "I swear, Maude!"

"Oh great, now you got Ruby swearing," Opal sighed.

"She didn't technically swear. She just said she swears. There's a big difference. Now, if we're talking about swearing, I know how to swear. I can teach you both how!" Maude laughed.

"No!" Ruby and Opal both retorted.

"Suit yourself," Maude shrugged. She took another quick taste of the icing when Ruby's back was turned, but Opal caught her out of the corner of her eye. "Ruby! She's doing it again!" Opal laughed.

"Maude, stop it! This is for the children!" Ruby reminded her.

"I know. I plan on buying it the moment it's up for grabs," Maude laughed. "I'm just making sure the product is adequate."

"Nobody bakes a cake better than Ruby Montgomery," Opal nodded.

"Thanks, Opal," Ruby smiled. "Now Maude, if you really want to help, wash those pans in the sink for me please. As soon as the cake comes out, we can adjust the temperature so Opal's cookies can go in."

"I'll wash those two pans and then ice the cake," Maude agreed.

"The cake will need to be cooled completely before it can be iced," Ruby explained.

"Whatever you say," Maude shrugged. She was too busy making mental notes of all the goodies she was going to buy the next afternoon. She loved this time of year when the local school held their annual bake sale fundraiser. She wasn't even sure where the funds were going to, but it didn't really matter. The fundraiser was the perfect time to stock her refrigerator and freezer with delicious pies, cakes, cookies, and treats.

"You know, for someone who loves sweets so much, you might as well finally learn how to bake," Ruby said.

"Why in the world would I ever do that?" Maude retorted. "You and Opal bake. Hell, even Nadine bakes. All y'all do, so I'm not needed. What do they say? That would be too many cooks in the kitchen," Maude smirked. "I know my way around the kitchen, but I don't need to bake when y'all do enough baking for the whole town practically."

"It might be a good skill to learn if you ever get married," Opal shrugged.

"I don't ever plan on getting married," Maude shook her head. "Plus, if a man only wants me because I can bake a cake, he ain't right for me."

"Whatever you say," Opal mocked Maude's earlier retort to Ruby.

"You're one to talk! Do you plan on getting married, Opal?" Maude asked.

"Who knows what lies in the future," Opal shrugged.

"Are y'all two done?" Ruby asked. "Opal, get those cookies on a sheet pan and be ready to put them in once I turn the oven back on to the right temperature."

"Aye aye," Opal saluted. She began to spoon the thick dough onto a greased sheet and made sure the cookies were evenly spaced.

"Alright, fingers crossed my cake looks alright," Ruby said. She took a deep breath and opened the oven door a tiny bit to peek inside. "Oh! It doesn't look too bad!"

"I'm sure it's perfect," Opal added.

"Always is," Maude agreed.

True to their thoughts, Ruby's cake was indeed perfect. She placed the warm cake pan on the counter on top of her favorite trivet. She adjusted the temperature on the stove and they waited for the oven's temperature to rise to the necessary temperature for Opal's cookies.

"What else is there to bake after all this?" Maude asked. She noted the cookies waiting to go into the oven, Ruby's uniced cake, the loaf of banana bread cooling in the window sill, and the chocolate pie she knew was in the refrigerator.

"Once the cookies are finished, I think we should be good to go," Opal announced.

"I don't know," Ruby fretted. "I want to make sure we have enough."

"There's always more than enough," Opal reminded her. "You aren't the only one responsible for this bake sale, remember?"

Ruby nodded. Sometimes she needed to be reminded that the weight of the world did not rest on her shoulders. Half of the women in Rhinestone had signed up to bake treats for the bake sale, so Opal was right.

"What time do you have to get all this up there?" Maude asked.

"They want everything ready to go by one o'clock tomorrow," Ruby noted. The bake sale was set to begin at two o'clock at the school. That would give everyone plenty of time to have finished church, eaten lunch, and arrive hungry for dessert. It was a rare event to have any leftovers at these kinds of fundraisers; the people of

Rhinestone loved any and everything with sugar, and they always supported one another.

The following afternoon had indeed turned into a festival of sorts. The desserts and treats had all been sorted by type. The cakes were showcased along two long tables that had been placed end to end. The circular table held platters of cookies, from chocolate chip to oatmeal raisin, iced sugar cookies in the shape of flowers to peanut butter blossoms. Another table held key lime pies, lemon custard pies, chocolate pies, peanut butter pies, chess pies, and one apple pie that Maude had her eye on. Yet another table had a few pans of various cobblers, fresh baked breads, and muffins galore: blueberry, chocolate chip, lemon poppyseed, banana nut, and strawberry. Each baker had priced their creations so that the buyers could gather up what they wanted and check out by the door.

The line was already forming when Maude arrived. She made a beeline for the tables with cakes, but she did not see Ruby's iced lemon pound cake anywhere. The other cakes looked delicious, but her heart was set on that iced lemon pound cake that Ruby wouldn't let her break off a small piece to taste last night. She looked over the three chocolate cakes that had been pushed closer to her by the smiling woman behind the counter who grinned. She was not hiding the fact that she wanted Maude to select all three of the cakes. "I don't want those," Maude sighed. "I'm looking for Ruby Montgomery's lemon pound cake."

"Oh, is this the one?" a voice behind her interrupted. Maude scowled and turned around to face Nadine Waters. She was holding Ruby's perfectly wrapped iced lemon pound cake. "I couldn't pass up one of Ruby's famous pound cakes," Nadine smiled.

"You've got to be kidding me," Maude snapped.

"Hey Maude!" Ruby said as she hurried towards them. "There you are! We've got a table over here. We've been waiting for you. Oh, hello, Nadine." It was then that she noticed which particular pound cake Nadine was holding.

"I hope you know that I stuck my finger in that cake and licked the spoon that I iced it with," Maude growled.

"No she didn't," Ruby assured Nadine. "Now Maude, you know that's not true. Let's go over here and let Nadine enjoy her cake." She quickly steered Maude away from the table of cakes.

"I hope she chokes on it," Maude mumbled underneath her breath.

"Maude! Don't say that!" Ruby chastised her. She pointed at the empty seat next to Melanie and motioned for Maude to sit down. "I'll make you your own lemon pound cake this evening if it's that big of a deal."

"Oh Lordy, what happened?" Jameson asked.

Maude recounted what happened with Nadine while Jameson struggled to hold back his laughter. "You know she did that on purpose," Maude frowned.

"How would she know that's the one you wanted?" Ruby asked.

"She just knows the worst way to irritate me. It's her calling in life, I swear," Maude sighed.

"I think it was just an unfortunate coincidence," Ruby explained. "You'll be fine. When you're good and calmed down, go walk over to the other tables and see what all's there."

"I'm fine. I'm not a child. Nadine's the child," Maude said. She asked Melanie if she wanted to walk to the tables with her and the little girl nodded enthusiastically. "Yes ma'am!"

"I better go, too," Ruby said. "Hold your horses, Maude!"

"Go on and make sure no one ends up in a fist fight," Jameson chuckled. "I'm off today." He patted his stomach and wiped his mouth with a napkin.

Ruby once again hurried off after Maude who was already selecting which cookies she wanted. "I'll take those right there," she pointed to a stack of peanut butter blossom cookies. She didn't see Opal's chocolate chip cookies on the table, but the peanut butter cookies looked perfectly fine. "Let me look at the pie table real fast and then I'll be ready to leave," Maude said to Ruby.

"This may be the cheapest bake sale you've ever attended," Ruby laughed. "I figured you'd load up on treats."

"I'm not in the mood," Maude said through gritted teeth. She looked over the pies left on the table and quickly selected a lemon pie and a blueberry pie. "Where do I check out?" she asked Ruby.

"Over there by the door," Ruby gestured to a table where Opal was sitting. Next to her was Nadine Waters. "Oh heavens," Ruby sighed inwardly.

"Hey Maude," Opal waved. "Wow, only three things? You feeling ok?"

"I'm fine," Maude said gruffly.

"No cake this year?" Nadine asked.

Maude took a deep breath and closed her eyes. Maybe if she counted to ten the feeling of wanting to throttle Nadine in front of everyone would dissipate.

Chapter Sixteen

Maude grimaced as Opal pulled a comb through her hair. She wasn't sure where all those knots had come from. She had worn a hat when she rode her motorcycle down the highway to get to the salon, and a hat was supposed to protect her hair from the wind. She hadn't slept well last night; she had tossed and turned nonstop while her dog grunted and sighed each time she apparently disturbed him. Who knew that dogs could sigh and whine like a human child!

"I'm going to have to bring out the big guns," Opal winced. She had been working on this one particular knot for ten minutes and short of cutting Maude's hair, she wasn't sure what else to do. There wasn't a product on the market that could smooth Maude's coarse hair. Not that Maude was particularly good at taking care of her hair either.

"The big guns?" Maude asked. She quickly looked around to make sure that Opal didn't really have a gun anywhere near her. Opal didn't own a gun, to her knowledge, but Ms. Belva probably had a few hidden around the shop. She was a notorious wild woman!

"I think I'm going to have to cut your hair,"

Opal fretted. "I don't know how you manage this every time, Maude. I have children who come in here with more manageable hair. Do you even own a brush?"

"Of course I do. Somewhere," Maude shrugged. "Oh hell, just go ahead and cut what you need and get me out of here. I have to drive over to Florence this afternoon and then back. My great-aunt Winifred is being honored for something and my parents said I have to go. The whole family is going. I've still got those old moldy letters and baseball cards she gave me. I don't know what I'm supposed to do with them, but mother said to get a move on with them."

Opal stared at the back of Maude's head and grimaced again. "How do you feel about going short?" she asked.

"How short?" Maude asked. Her hair wasn't long by any means; it was shorter than Ruby's shoulder length hair that she often wore in a loose bun, yet longer than Opal's hair that she always kept perfectly styled.

"I'm talking a wavy pixie cut here," Opal said.

"I have no idea what any of those words mean," Maude countered.

Opal sighed and rolled her eyes. "You know what a wave is," she motioned her hands like the rippling of a wave. "And a pixie, like, you know, short," Opal continued.

"I don't want to be bald," Maude said.

"Nowhere in my explanation did I say the word bald," Opal sighed. "I just don't think you are capable of or responsible enough to manage your hair. I'm going to have to treat you like a child who gets candy stuck in their hair. Maude! Are you seriously unwrapping candy while I chastise you?"

Maude snickered and popped the piece of candy in her mouth. "Just do what you have to do. I have places to be and people to see."

"Alright, but don't you dare complain once I get started or when you see the end results. I'm a professional, but sometimes a client comes along that is just unreasonable, and if there ever was one," Opal trailed off.

"Yea, yea, yea," Maude said. She wasn't necessarily keen on going any shorter, but she was on a time crunch and really didn't have the time to be driving to Florence and back in one afternoon, but her family had been adamant that she not miss this big shindig for her great- aunt Winifred. Winifred Cooper had been dead for over thirteen years, but the town was just now dedicating a fountain in one of their city parks to her. Maude had no idea why. Great-aunt Winifred was a stingy old lady who rarely left her house in the center of town. She had no children of her own, but she had promised to leave her fortune to the first child in the family to bear her name. "I don't know why I have to go all the way to Florence for this thing. Opal, are you even listening to me? I'm complaining about that crazy old coot left me a pack of baseball cards and some ol' moldy letters and now I'm stuck with a middle name like Winifred," Maude grumbled, but Opal was too busy deciding which pair of scissors to use on Maude's hair.

It wasn't the worst name. Maude's brother had also been named in honor of their great-aunt. He had been christened Maurice Muriel, since she was Winifred Muriel. Maude had gotten out easy with Maude Winifred. Great-aunt Winifred had been thrilled and vowed to leave her fortune to both Maude and Maurice, but neither had seen such fortune. Maurice had gotten the old lady's house, but he sold it quickly as he preferred to live in Junction, not Florence. Maude had inherited four small boxes of baseball cards and a box of letters with strings wrapped around them. She had never taken anything out of the boxes, even though Ruby and Opal had been mighty curious over the years. Maybe this was a sign to finally see what was in the boxes.

"Ok, what do you think?" Opal asked finally. She handed Maude a hand mirror and bit her lip as Maude frowned. "It's shorter than you said," Maude all but shouted.

"To be fair, I never gave you a direct number. I had to do my best with what I was given," Opal retorted. "I think it looks great. You'll be the talk of the town with this new style. Oh, and you're welcome."

"I'm usually the talk of the town," Maude admitted. "Sure, thanks, I'll get used to it. Now hand me my hat so I can get this over with."

"You can't wear a hat!" Opal shrieked. All heads turned towards Opal from the waiting area. "Maude, I just worked my literal magic on your head and you are not going to cover it up and get us back in the same mess we were just in."

"Opal, I have to ride my motorcycle to Florence and back. My hair is just going to be whatever it is," Maude explained. She handed Opal some money and smiled at Belva who was flitting between two different clients in her section of the salon. "I'll call you when I get home and tell you all about the drama in Florence," Maude called over her shoulder to Opal as she bounced out the front door. She hopped on her motorcycle, pulled her baseball cap down over her ears, and took off down the highway towards Florence.

"Well, color me crazy," Opal said to Ms. Belva who found the whole situation hysterical. "She's got a style all her own. That's for sure."

Two hours later, Maude peeled into the parking lot of one of the local gas stations in Florence. She was starving, but she was already running late. She was supposed to meet her parents and Maurice at the park, but she couldn't remember where it was. It had been quite a few years since she had been anywhere near Florence. She gassed up her bike and stopped inside to see what food offerings the station had. She was pleasantly surprised to see the roller food was up to her standards. She downed a soda and two hotdogs before asking the gas station attendant if he knew where a ceremony was being held in one of the local parks today. He pointed her in the right direction and off she went.

She knew she was in the right place before she parked because she saw her dad's blue truck pulled onto the grassy knoll. There was a decent crowd standing around a small fountain that shot water straight up into the air in the center of a pool. A newspaper crew was there snapping photographs and someone who Maude presumed to be of importance was giving a speech. The man was sweating from the heat in his long sleeved black shirt and black pants. She could see beads of sweat dripping off the end of his nose. Her mother and father were standing next to the man smiling, but they, too, looked hot in the bright sunshine. Maude's brother, Maurice, was standing off to the side. He caught Maude's eye and beckoned her to hurry. "You're late," he laughed quietly as she sidled up next to him. "And what did you do to your hair?"

"Don't ask," Maude hissed. "What are we doing here anyway?"

"Apparently great-aunt Winifred left the city some money. I guess they had to wait a certain amount of time before it could be theirs, but it sounds like it was a pretty good piece. Maybe I should've kept the house after all," he chuckled.

"So they bought a fountain?" Maude asked.

"From what the mayor said, they spent the money on some new playground equipment. I guess the fountain is part of it. I don't really know. It's too hot out here for me to listen. And I'm starving," Maurice added.

"Let's get something to eat after this. I'll need all the energy for the drive back. That was probably the most boring drive I've ever done," Maude said.

"Yea, there ain't much between here and Rhinestone," he nodded. He looked at his watch and shuffled his feet. "He's been going nonstop for fifteen minutes now. How much can you say about some water and an old recluse?"

A few minutes later the heat won out. The mayor shook a few hands and quickly walked to the nearest building which must be where his offices were located. Maude's parents spoke to people in the crowd and slowly made their way over to their children. "That sure was something!" Maude's father said. "Now let's get something to eat. I haven't eaten all day. What do you say?"

"That was it?" Maude asked. "I drove two hours for that?"

"It's for family," Maude's mother spoke softly.

"She's been dead for over a decade," Maude gasped.

"Shh," her mother shushed her. "Lord, let's get you two fed before you float away. We can have a nice meal and then make the drive back. I admit it was a little strange that they insisted we be here, but great-aunt Winifred did a lot for this town and for us."

Winifred had indeed left quite a bit of money to her only nephew, Maude's father. They were able to pay off their business debts and take a vacation to the Grand Canyon, somewhere Maude's mother had always wanted to see. After a lively late lunch at one of Florence's local barbecue joints, they all parted ways. Maurice needed to get back to Junction, but Maude's parents had decided to spend the night in Florence and venture back home the next day. They had an afternoon of antiquing, or picking as her dad referred to it, on the schedule. They tried to get Maude to stay, but she reminded them that she needed to feed the dog and finish Lester Picken's old Chevy that needed a tune up.

The drive back to Rhinestone wasn't terrible. She pulled into the mechanic's garage and made quick work of Mr. Picken's pickup truck. Mr. Pickens babied his old truck and took great care of it, so there was never any big issue that needed attention. Maude was exhausted from the adventures of the day, so she tidied up the shop and drove over yonder to the Piggly Wiggly to see if they still had any of their fried chicken left. Thankfully, they did, because she was not in the mood to cook this evening. As soon as she got home, she tore into the fried chicken and mashed potatoes with gravy. She peeked out her front window and saw Opal pulling into her driveway. With a yawn and a big stretch, Maude stood up and walked outside to see if Opal wanted to come over and help her go through the boxes in the spare bedroom.

"Opal!" Maude shouted, causing Opal to drop the box she was holding.

"What in the world is wrong with you?" Opal called back. "Never mind! The list is far too long to go over."

Maude moseyed her way across the small field in between the two houses. She hoped that the box Opal had been carrying didn't have anything breakable in it. Opal hand picked up the box and had taken it inside her house by the time she arrived on her porch. "You bellowed?" Opal said at the door.

"I was just trying to get your attention," Maude

laughed. "What was in the box?"

"Wigs," Opal said nonchalantly.

"I don't even want to know," Maude held up her hands.

"How was your event thing in Florence? I'm surprised you're already back," Opal said.

Maude told her all about the quick turnaround and how it felt like a waste of time. She did enjoy lunch with her brother and parents, but she could eat with them any old time. "So, you want to help me go through those old boxes or not?" Maude finished.

"I can help you," Opal nodded. "Have you eaten supper yet? What am I asking? Of course you have. I'm going to make a salad before I head over. Do you want one?"

Maude shook her head and waited for Opal to make her way to her kitchen and find what all kinds of rabbit food she wanted to make her salad with. She recognized the carrots and some kind of lettuce, but she was lost at whatever else Opal tossed into the bowl. As soon as Opal was satisfied, she followed Maude across the field to Maude's house where they could hear the television blaring. "You left it on?" Opal asked.

"Buford was watching it," Maude shrugged.

"A dog watching television," Opal chuckled. "Oh goodness, when was the last time you cleaned in here?" She stepped over Maude's work boots that were in the doorway and looked around the messy living room.

"I'll get to it directly," Maude shrugged. She disappeared into the back room and reemerged a few minutes later balancing a stack of boxes on top of each other. She set them precariously on the cluttered coffee table and sank down on the couch. Opal made room next to her and looked at Maude to direct her where to start. "I guess we'll start with this box," she said as she picked up the smaller of the boxes on top. She made a slit through the tape with her pocket knife and opened the flaps. "Yep, baseball cards."

Opal pulled out a few of the cards on top and gasped. "Oh my heavens," she breathed. "Maude, these are not just baseball cards. These are baseball royalty."

Maude pulled the box closer to her and her eyes widened. Ted Williams, Joe DiMaggio, Babe Ruth, and Jackie Robinson stared back at her in pristine condition. "What in the treasure trove is all this?" she gasped.

Chapter Seventeen

"Hey, Ruby! Can I talk to Jameson?" Maude asked in one breath. She held the receiver up to her ear and huffed and puffed.

"Maude? Are you ok? What's going on?" Ruby asked. She gripped the phone and all but gasped, waiting for Maude to answer.

"I'm fine. I just need to talk to Jameson. He knows about these kinds of things," Maude rushed on. Ruby could hear Opal in the background saying, "Wow. I can't believe this" over and over again.

"Maude? Opal? What is going on?" Ruby asked again. Her nerves were shot.

"I need to talk to Jameson," Maude repeated. "Shh, Opal, I can't hear anything with you carrying on like that!" Opal had pushed her face close to the receiver and shouted hello to Ruby as Maude swatted her away.

Ruby set the phone down and hollered for Jameson who came running into the kitchen less than thirty seconds later. "What's going on? Are you ok? Who died?" Jameson shouted.

"I don't know. Maude's on the phone and said she needs to talk to you!" Ruby exclaimed, wide eyed and nearly out of breath. Her heart was racing fast. "And Opal's there but I can't make out what all she's saying. I hope she isn't hurt. Oh heavens, ask where they are! Do I need to get the car? Melanie, come down here!" Ruby's mind quickly went to the worst of the worst. Jameson was a renowned lawyer, so surely that was why her best friends were calling. Maude had even said that Jameson was an expert in such matters.

Jameson picked up the phone and held the receiver to his ear. "Hello? Is everything alright? Where are you?"

Ruby pressed her face as close to Jameson as possible, but she could not hear anything that Maude was saying. She tried to read Jameson's face, but as always, he was stoic as he nodded and listened.

"What's going on?" Ruby whispered, but Jameson shook his head. He was trying to understand what Maude was rambling about. He caught something about baseball, Willie Mays, Sandy Koufax, and some old letters. "Jameson! What is going on?" Ruby asked again. Did they not realize that they were making her more anxious by ignoring her!

"Maude, I'll be right there," Jameson said into the phone. He hastily hung up the phone and kissed Ruby on the cheek. "This shouldn't take long. Or maybe it will. I don't know. I'll be back soon."

"Jameson Bertram Montgomery, what on earth is going on?" Ruby demanded. She had her hands on her hips and she looked fierce in her pink paisley apron.

"Oh, mama said your full name," Melanie gasped from the doorway.

"Everything is ok, I promise," Jameson said. He grinned his devilish grin that softened Ruby's hard exterior. "Maude's got some baseball cards she wants me to look at."

"Baseball cards?" Ruby huffed. "Baseball cards? Are you? Baseball cards!"

Jameson wrapped his arms around his wife and hugged her tightly. He kissed the top of her head and said, "Why don't you and Melanie load up in the car and we'll all go see about these baseball cards."

"I'm going to whoop you all once I get there," Ruby grumbled. They had gotten her heart rate up over some silly baseball cards. It was like Maude and Jameson were both kids at heart when it came to baseball cards of all things. Ruby understood and even appreciated the fact that both Jameson and Maude liked to follow the happenings in baseball, but there was no need to get all up in a tizzy over some pieces of paper. She was thankful that Maude hadn't been involved in any kind of danger or scandal, but Lord have mercy, she was going to give them all a talking to!

As soon as the Montgomery family pulled onto the grass in front of Maude's house, Maude flew down the porch steps and met Jameson at the driver's side window. She was giddy with excitement. Ruby wasn't sure the last time she saw Maude in such a state of excitement. "Oh, Ruby, you came, too. Hi Melanie! Hurry up, Jameson!

This can't wait!" Maude all but drug Jameson into her house by his arm.

Melanie stopped on the porch to pet Maude's old dog who had fallen asleep next to a pair of muddy boots. "I better check on them inside," Ruby told Melanie, who was content letting the dog lick her face as he wagged his tail. "Yes ma'am," Melanie giggled.

Ruby opened the front door and found Maude, Jameson, and Opal gathered around the coffee table in the living room. "What's the meaning of all this?" Ruby asked.

"I've found buried treasure!" Maude exclaimed. She had a wild look in her eye and a grin plastered across her face.

"It wasn't buried," Opal countered. "Well, unless you count buried in a box in Maude's junk room. Then maybe so."

"Buried treasure?" Ruby asked.

"I'm sitting on a gold mine," Maude said. "A literal gold mine."

"I don't think Maude knows exactly what the term literal means when referring to a goldmine, but for all intents and purposes, metaphorically of course, this could potentially be a gold mine," Opal nodded.

"What?" Ruby asked. Her head was already spinning.

"This could actually be worth quite a fortune," Jameson said. He was shocked at what was before him on the table.

"I told you!" Maude nodded emphatically.

"Nobody's arguing with you," Opal laughed.

She turned to wink at Ruby who still wore an expression of bewilderment across her face. "Oh, Ruby, let me catch you up! You remember that old box of stuff from Maude's aunt Winifred? Well, here it is. Maude finally decided to open it and see what was inside. Surprise, surprise! It appears to be a goldmine."

"All I see are some baseball cards," Ruby said.

"Ah, but the kinds of cards are the prize," Opal pointed out. "You have to look beyond the physical card and see the value attached."

"Opal's right. These are very rare, and they aren't cheap. Looks like your aunt was in fact sitting on a small goldmine. I really can't believe it," Jameson explained.

"All this time you've had what could amount to a fortune in your spare room?" Ruby asked.

"Looks that way," Opal chuckled. "She could've sold them years ago, but then again they might not have had the value that they do now. No one knows."

"You could always keep them," Jameson offered suddenly.

Ruby and Opal both snapped their attention towards Maude and studied her face. "I could," Maude mused. "But they'd probably go right back in a box and I might lose them. Or the dog could eat them. Or if there's a fire. There's too many what ifs. I think I'll see what I can get for them. They aren't doing me any good sitting in an old box. They are really nice though."

"Or she might forget about them again and let them keep collecting value," Opal nodded.

"Exactly," Jameson agreed.

Maude had never been the type of person to collect anything. Some people had expensive stamp collections, doll collections, rocks, and buttons and pins. None of that ever intrigued Maude, but she could always start her own collection of rare and expensive baseball cards. Ruby was the one in the friend group that had a propensity to collect things. Jameson referred to it as hoarding, but Ruby was neat and kept everything organized. She never met a gift shop or antique store that she did not immediately fall in love with.

"Earth to Ruby," Opal laughed. She snapped her fingers in front of Ruby to get her attention. "Maude's decided to sell the cards to the highest bidder. Jameson is going to help her. To celebrate, prematurely I might add, Maude wants to eat ice cream. Do you want any?"

"Do you ever take a breath when you ramble?" Maude asked hastily. "Anyway, who wants ice cream?"

Everyone of course wanted some ice cream. Maude scooped each person a generous portion of chocolate ice cream from a large carton in her freezer. "Not a vegetable in sight," Opal lamented as she peeked in the freezer and bottom refrigerator. "It wouldn't kill you to add some natural greens to your diet. The more colorful the food, the healthier you are."

"What do you think these are for?" Maude asked. She showed Opal the three other cartons of ice cream in her freezer next to the chocolate.

"Strawberry, butter pecan, and fudge swirl? Not the colors I was referring to. I'm talking carrots, squash, collards and mustard greens. Even a banana, apple, or pear, something to shock your system besides the constant sugar and carbohydrates you're always downing," Opal sighed.

"I'm right as rain," Maude shrugged. "Finer than the vine."

"It's fine as wine," Opal corrected her.

"Whatever," Maude stuck her tongue out at Opal. Melanie giggled as she ate her ice cream. It was never a dull moment at Maude's house or anywhere where Maude was.

"We need to find someone whose expertise is in baseball card collections," Jameson said in between mouthfuls. "I can ask around, but your best bet is to contact someone in Atlanta or somewhere like that."

"I know a guy," Opal nodded. "He's out of Atlanta, but we can make it over there and back pretty fast if you drive."

"Does this man have a name?" Maude asked. She raised her eyebrows in consternation.

"Of course he has a name," Opal scoffed. "Everyone has a name. Geez, Maude." Jameson, Maude, Ruby, and Melanie all stared at Opal from their seats waiting for her to go on. "What?" Opal asked. She was used to people staring at her, but usually she was doing something worth staring at, not merely eating an apple.

"What's his name?" Maude roared.

"Wow, calm down there, partner," Opal said.

"You get all worked up over nothing. His name is Boxy."

"Boxy?" Ruby repeated. She was afraid she had heard Opal wrong.

"Yes, Boxy," Opal nodded.

"I'm almost afraid to ask," Maude sighed. "Opal, why is this man called Boxy? And if you tell me that's what his mama named him, I'm going to scream."

"You really need to settle down, Maude. His government name is Theodore, but he lives in a box down by the river," Opal explained. She was clearly exasperated always having to explain things to Maude. Not that Maude had probably ever heard of Boxy before, but the details of his name were not important to the issue at hand.

"Oh, well now that makes sense," Maude said sarcastically. She rolled her eyes and shrugged her shoulders at Ruby. "Boxy, of course! Why didn't I think of that!"

"He's a genius when it comes to things like this," Opal continued.

"Um, Opal, why exactly is he living in a box by the river?" Ruby asked gently.

"He likes it, I guess," Opal shrugged. She had never asked Boxy why he lived in a box near the boat dock in the outskirts of Atlanta. He was a very nice, quiet man who had grown up wanting nothing more than to be a professor of higher education, but when the draft began, he was one of the first snatched from his dreams. He traded in his briefcase and red pen that he used to grade papers for a gun and a lingering shoulder issue that would haunt him for the rest of his life. His short stint as a helicopter gunner left him with nothing but horrific memories and a constant fear of loud noises and people. He much preferred his box and the gentle sounds of nature. Opal had met Boxy at one of the dinners down at the veterans center. He had come with Lefty, a man who was missing his left arm. Lefty loved to dance and constantly whistled a tune loudly when he walked into a room. He introduced Opal to his friend who had gone by Theo at that point, but not long after a few more of those dinners, Theo had moved to the outskirts of Atlanta and had become known as Boxy, his new moniker thrust upon him by Lefty who had followed him out there a few times.

"He's a genius," Opal explained. "He just, well, like so many of them, he just didn't come back the same. I haven't seen him in quite some time, but I imagine I know where to find him. How many men named Boxy live near the Yellow River near Atlanta?"

"I'm not so sure about this," Ruby whispered to Maude and Jameson, but Jameson shook his head. "Opal knows what she's doing. Alright, most of the time," he chuckled.

"It's always an adventure," Opal grinned. "I'll get up with Lefty this evening and see if he wants to go along with us. What do you say, Maude? Take off tomorrow and let's go on an adventure. Ruby has to be the responsible one this time, but if you're feeling ill, Ruby, you can come, too." Opal winked at Melanie who had been absorbing this conversation the whole time. They both knew that

Ruby would never fake sick to get out of anything.

"I expect a full debriefing of said adventure as soon as y'all return home," Ruby instructed. She knew she would worry about them both the entire time they were gone. That's just how it was with friends.

Jameson chuckled again and motioned for Melanie to follow him back to the living room so he could look at the baseball cards once more. Melanie left her mother and Maude and Opal gabbing at the kitchen table about their plans and followed her father to Maude's living room. "What's in this box?" Melanie asked. She pointed to a box that was ripped along one side. Maude had shoved it underneath the coffee table in her excitement of discovering the baseball cards.

"I'm not sure," Jameson answered. "Hey, Maude, what about this other box?"

Maude peeked around the corner and noticed the box Jameson was referring to. "It's just a bunch of old letters. I haven't really looked at them. Y'all are welcome to go through them if you want."

Jameson winked at Melanie and they both immediately convened on the box in question. Now that they had Maude's permission, their intrigue had been more than piqued. "What's that smell?" Melanie asked as she wrinkled her nose.

"Age," Jameson replied. "That's the smell of time passing. Some call it memories."

"It smells like cigarette smoke and stale cardboard," Melanie said.

"Yes, I imagine some memories do smell like cigarette smoke," Jameson nodded. "Let's see what this is all about." He carefully lifted the first bundle of letters from the top of the stack. The pages were folded and tied together with a faded ribbon. "This is mighty old, indeed," Jameson surmised. He untied the ribbon carefully and unfolded the first letter. "I'll be!" he gasped.

"What is it?" Melanie asked, wide-eyed.

"This is dated 1861," Jameson said softly. He read the letter in his hand until he got to the last line. "Maude, you might want to come in here," he said a little louder.

"Everything ok?" Maude asked.

"Oh, yes," Jameson replied. "But I think the baseball cards are the least of your treasures."

Chapter Eighteen

"Change of plans," Maude breathed quietly. "Change of plans! Forget the baseball cards. These letters are from the Civil War!" She had a stack of letters in her lap and looked up at the faces staring back at her intently. "These are the new gold mines."

Maude, Opal, and Ruby had joined Melanie and Jameson back in the living room at Jameson's request. They had all begun to read the letters voraciously, as carefully as they could.

"Who are they from?" Melanie squinted at the small, dainty writing on the letter she held in her hand. The words on the paper were all written in cursive and were dainty and small. She had never seen such neat handwriting before.

"From someone named Elizabeth. It looks like she's writing to someone named William. I don't know who William and Elizabeth are though," Maude answered. "They would have to be somebody in my family, I think, because why else would my aunt Winifred have these? It can't be Winifred's parents because their names were something weird. Elizabeth and William are too common for my family."

"That sounds about right. Call your mom and see if she knows," Opal suggested.

"I can't get up with them right now. They're still in Florence. I don't think my brother would know either. Do you think your aunt Willie might know something?" Maude asked Opal.

"Aunt Willie knows everything about everybody," Opal nodded. She went back to reading the letter in her hand.

"Opal! Call her. Time is of the essence!" Maude barked. She was over stimulated and over eager about this new potentially lucrative path.

"Well, there's one little problem," Opal replied calmly. She kept her eyes glued to the letter she had been reading.

"What's the problem?" Maude asked, tersely.

"I don't really know where she's at right now. Last I heard she was headed to California for a spell, but I'm not sure when she's coming back. You know she likes to go where the wind blows her. I wish I could be like that," Opal mused.

"You are just like her," Maude chuckled.

"These letters have to be worth something," Jameson interjected. "Maude, do you have any other random boxes in that old room?"

Maude shook her head. "These are it, I think. I wonder if some of the museums might be interested in taking a look at these old letters. What do you think?"

"I think they would absolutely be interested in these," Jameson nodded. "Are you sure there's no other boxes?"

Maude shrugged, but decided to check just

in case. She returned to the living room a few minutes later with two more boxes. "Ok, these are the last ones. Promise!" she grinned.

Jameson helped her open the top box and gasped. The box was full of both Union and Confederate money, sketches of battlefields, folded battle flags, an engraved pocket watch, and what had to be a copy of the Terms of Surrender letter signed by Confederate General Robert E. Lee himself. Jameson caught his breath and became unsteady on his feet. "Maude, this is, this can't be," he gasped. "Oh good heavens!"

"What is it?" Maude asked.

"I can't believe it," Jameson said. He handed Maude the document and watched as recognition dawned on her. "Oh. My. God." She handed the paper to Opal who then passed it to Ruby.

"Good heavens!" Ruby heaved. "Maude, you've had literal pieces of history in your spare room all this time!"

"I can't believe this," Maude repeated. She sank down in the couch and held onto the paper tightly. Opal, Ruby, and Jameson continued to look through the remaining box and pulled out a Confederate uniform with brass buttons. It was in near perfect condition, complete with a small knife wrapped in the folds of the pants.

After Maude came out of her daze, Jameson counted the letters one by one as he tied them back together and stacked them back in their respective box. There were fifty-seven letters in all, most of them written by someone named Elizabeth to a William. There were a handful of letters from

William back to Elizabeth, but they were brief from the battlefield. "The one from the battle of Shiloh is incredible," Jameson continued. "Shiloh was a major battle. It was the bloodiest battle up until that point. I can't imagine the things that William would have seen."

The plan to find Boxy and have him assess the baseball cards was quickly scrapped in favor of having a museum take a look at the letters and memorabilia. The nearest museum that would possibly have an interest in the letters was in Birmingham, which wasn't too far of a drive. Maude and Opal decided to waste no time and set out early in the morning towards Birmingham with an extra pep in their step. Ruby couldn't help but think of them all day as she taught her students. When the clock struck the end of the work day, she gathered up her papers and waited for Melanie to walk down to her classroom. When they got home, Ruby began prepping for dinner while Melanie hurried through her homework. Jameson arrived promptly a few minutes after five-thirty that afternoon asking if Ruby had heard from either of her friends, but she shook her head.

The family had dinner together and Melanie went upstairs to get ready for bed. Ruby was getting more worried by the minute, but she wouldn't say anything aloud so as not to worry Melanie or Jameson. Once Melanie was safely tucked in bed, Jameson and Ruby retired to the living room to read the newspaper and grade papers respectfully. They continued on in silence for thirty minutes until the phone rang, causing

Ruby to jump slightly. Jameson walked to the kitchen and answered the phone on the wall. Ruby had followed behind him and heard the levity in his voice. He handed the phone to her and sat down at the table to listen.

Ruby was relieved to hear the excitement in their voices on the other end of the line. From what she gathered, the visit to the museum had gone better than expected. The museum was very interested in procuring the letters, but there was now a bidding war that could potentially involve the Smithsonian in Washington D.C.

The next few days passed quickly with Maude being invited to Washington D.C. along with her letters. "This is big time!" Jameson cheered when he heard the news, but Maude wasn't convinced. She did not want to hop on a plane by herself for any amount of money. Maude had never been a fan of flying. She much preferred to keep her feet on the ground. With Jameson's help, she was able to arrange meetings between the brokers in Washington for a deal. The Smithsonian offered to display the letters and memorabilia with a plaque stating whom the donation was from, but Maude and her team of lawyers were not budging. They were offering a direct sale of the memorabilia, letters, and documents for a certain price. Ruby had been shocked by the number on the piece of paper indicating the price Maude and her team were asking for, but Jameson assured her that the bulk of the materials were more than worth the price tag.

After two weeks of haggling, the museum

sent their own representative to verify the items, and to their satisfaction, everything checked out. Once they were in possession of the items, they sent a certified money order for the total asking price to Maude's bank of choice.

"You're rich!" Opal cheered over a celebratory glass of champagne.

"Yes, I am," Maude burped. She had never been a fan of the bubbly stuff, but Opal had brought over the champagne and toasted her repeatedly. She wasn't sure if it was possible to get buzzed from such a weak drink, but the two of them had breezed through the bottle effortlessly. As Maude thought over what she wanted to do with her new found fortune, she realized that she was already living the life of her dreams. She had a house that was more than enough for her and her dog, enough land for the dog to run around on, and a motorcycle. She didn't have a long list of wants or needs like other people she knew who had come into money before, so she decided to invest it. Hopefully, it would continue to do what she needed it to do and she could retire early. She loved her job, but it wasn't something that she wanted to do until she died.

"Well, some of us still have to work for a living," Opal chuckled. She rinsed out the glass bottle and dried it with the towel by Maude's kitchen sink. "Do you need an empty bottle for anything? If not, I'll take it home."

"You can have it," Maude answered. She yawned loudly which startled the dog who had curled up beneath her feet. "I feel like I could sleep for days."

Opal chuckled and tucked the bottle under her arm. "I'll see you later," she smiled and slipped outside into the night air. She was happy for Maude, but something had been nagging her all day. There was a sharp chill in the air that was out of character for this time of year, but Opal shrugged it off and picked up Leo, her favorite cat, who was waiting dutifully by the front door.

"Ciao, Leo. È ora di andare a dormire," Opal soothed the cranky cat. She was convinced that he only spoke Italian, which was fitting since he was a rescue from Italy. Opal had snuck him into her purse when she, Ruby, and Maude left Italy eleven years ago after a wild vacation turned adventure. Leo was the souvenir of a lifetime. Leo purred and rubbed his face against Opal's chest as she carried him into her bedroom.

Opal awoke early the next morning after a fitful night of sleep. She had tossed and turned all night long, which was quite unusual. Leo had long given up on her and had retreated hastily to the living room where he wouldn't be accidentally kicked off the bed again. The phone in the kitchen rang, interrupting the meditations Opal was in the middle of. She did the same meditations every morning before she rolled out of bed in order to help her focus on the day ahead of her, but this morning was already proving difficult. The phone continued to ring until she picked it up and mumbled, "Opal speaking." The voice on the other end didn't wait for her to finish before launching into news that would certainly change

Opal's life.

One door down, Maude was dreaming of swimming in an Olympic sized swimming pool full of champagne as gold coins rained down. She awoke with a start as Buford barked and growled at the front door. Who on earth would be at her front door at this time of day! Maude threw on her robe and made her way to the front door where Buford was standing guard. She peeked out the peep hole and saw Opal standing in front of the door crying softly. Maude threw open the door and yanked Opal inside. "Opal! What's wrong? What's going on?"

Opal walked inside and sat down on the couch. Buford had stopped barking at the sight of Opal and jumped up in her lap. Opal absentmindedly patted him on the top of his head and sighed deeply. "Thomas is dead," she whispered.

"Thomas? Your cousin Thomas?" Maude asked. She was still not fully awake. Opal nodded, and Maude continued asking questions. "How do you know?"

Opal explained that her mother had called her this morning. Thomas' mother, Vivianne, had received the news last night when an Army chaplain showed up at her front door. Opal's mother was packing a bag to head to Tennessee to stay with her big sister and help her plan the funeral. Thomas had been struck down by a sniper's bullet and his body would be returning to the United States on the next transport. When she had more news, she would phone Opal and give her details.

Maude sat next to her dearest friend and patted her hand as she spoke. Maude was at a loss for words on how best to comfort Opal. She could tell that Opal had not slept well, so she offered to make them both some coffee. She slipped into the kitchen and dialed Ruby's house. She knew it was early and Ruby was probably sound asleep still on this Saturday morning, but she would want to know. Jameson answered and Maude quickly told him what was going on. He promised to wake Ruby and send her over as soon as she could get dressed. "Tell Opal I am so sorry to hear this. We will be praying for her and for all of Thomas' family during this terrible time," Jameson added.

Maude waited for the machine to finish brewing the coffee and then poured the hot black liquid into two mugs. She handed the bright yellow one with white daisies on it to Opal who murmured thanks as she stared out the window watching the birds chirp as they flew by. "It's crazy how life goes on," she whispered quietly.

"What do you mean?" Maude asked. She sipped the steaming cup of bitter coffee slowly, careful as not to burn her tongue.

"Look at the birds. No care in the world. The wind is still blowing, the sun is shining," Opal mused. "Time doesn't ever stop, even if I wished it would, even if only for a second. I can't believe he's gone. There's so many, Maude. There's so many of them just gone."

All Maude could do was nod. She had seen the staggering number of dead and wounded on the nightly news. There had been over forty thousand deaths attributed to the Vietnam War thus far, and there would surely be more to come. The men who had come back home alive were not always in the most fit or right shape. Opal had once said that many had come back haunted, and Maude knew what she meant. There was a certain way about them that did indeed look like they were constantly being haunted by the ghosts of the jungle battlefields.

It didn't take Ruby long to get dressed and drive to Maude's house. Maude met her at the door and hugged her tightly. "She's ok, well, as best as can be expected. This ain't her first rodeo when it comes to bad news in this war," Maude whispered. Ruby nodded and smiled gently at Opal who met her eye. Ruby sat down next to Opal and pulled her in for a tight hug. "We're all in this together. Always have been, always will be. Now and forever," Ruby reminded her.

Chapter Nineteen

Less than two weeks later Opal packed up her car to head to Memphis. The night before, Maude asked her for the eleventh time if she wanted her to tag along. Even though Maude already knew that Opal would want to undertake this trip alone, she still asked. That's what friends did, after all.

Opal pulled onto a long stretch of highway and thought out loud. She was alone in the car, but talking out loud helped calm her nerves. She was well aware that many people thought her a bit odd, but she did not care. The sky was still dusky, the kind of morning where the world held its breath, as if waiting for something to happen. Opal had known something terrible was on the horizon, even before she'd gotten the call. She could feel in her bones that something was about to happen. Her cousin had died. Not in the way he deserved after growing old, happily surrounded by family and friends. He deserved peace, but instead he was killed in the broad daylight in the jungle. This wasn't just another loss in a distant war—it was her family, and the ripple of grief would affect everyone.

A mortar shell, the kind that seemed to come

out of nowhere, had torn through his unit, ending his life instantly. The Army had sent the telegram to his mother, Ruth, but the notification had been passed along to Opal's mother, Thomas' aunt, because Ruth had been too distraught to speak, too broken to comprehend the enormity of the loss. Thomas had always been a bright light in his mother's eye, and now, in the blink of an eye, he was gone.

The day before, Ruth had called Opal in a voice so thin with sorrow it almost didn't sound like her. She had asked Opal to come to Memphis for the funeral. "I need you, Opal," Ruth had said, the words full of a quiet pleading that Opal couldn't ignore. And so, without hesitation, Opal had packed her small suitcase yet again, grabbed a handful of tissues, and got behind the wheel of her car, setting her course northward.

The journey from Montgomery to Memphis, Tennessee, wasn't an exceptionally long one— around four hours, depending on traffic. But to Opal , it felt like she was traveling through an eternity of grief. The road stretched before her like a ribbon of asphalt, leading her to a destination she never wanted to reach. The morning air, heavy with the scent of the warm earth and dew-covered grass, was a sharp contrast to the gnawing emptiness in her chest. She could feel the pulse of her sorrow, not in her limbs, but deep in her bones.

Opal knew this trip well. She had driven these roads countless times, passing through the small towns and sleepy stretches of land between

Rhinestone and Memphis. Her extended family lived in Memphis, and Ms. Belva had many a client in Memphis, too. Opal had often visited, but this was different. The landscape seemed to take on a heavier, more oppressive feeling. The rolling hills of Alabama seemed to weigh down on her as she passed through the rural towns and gas stations. The radio played softly, but every song seemed to echo the sadness that settled like a fog in her mind.

Her thoughts drifted back to the last time she had heard Thomas' voice. It was Christmas of 1969. Thomas had come home for a short visit, and Opal remembered how his laugh sparkled with hopefully optimism on the other end of the phone. He had been so eager to talk about his experience in Vietnam, and Opal had listened with a mixture of pride and fear. His stories were filled with bravado and humor—he made light of the hardships, as most young men did in an attempt to hide the fear that accompanied their service. But deep down, Opal had known the truth. She had heard the way Thomas' voice trembled when he talked about losing his best friend, the way his voice flickered nervously when the sound of a car backfiring echoed too loudly in the room. But he never spoke of it. Instead, he kept his stories light, as though keeping the darkness at bay through sheer force of will. Now, she would never have the chance to ask him about it. The light in Thomas' eyes would never return. All she had left were memories and a long drive to a funeral.

The car rumbled steadily along the highway as Opal passed through small towns like Jasper and

Hamilton, the dusty roads lined with homes that looked as though they hadn't changed in years. She passed the landmarks of her own past—places she'd once visited with her parents as a child and young adult, towns that had seen their fair share of hardship and joy, towns that were still recovering from the wounds of the Civil Rights Movement. It was as though the history of this region, with its deep roots in both war and peace, was woven into every mile of road she crossed. She had been in and out of these towns over the years, though she didn't often talk about it. Few people knew that she had been part of the resistance, long before the laws had been changed and enforced. She would continue to be part of the resistance, however that looked, for as long she had breath in her lungs.

The radio crackled as Opal adjusted the dial, and a soft country song played through the speakers. "Leaving on a Jet Plane" by John Denver filled the car. The familiar melody seemed to wrap around her, and for a moment, she closed her eyes, letting the sound wash over her. The song reminded her of so many brave men and women who were living out the words of the haunting song, only to be enveloped by the war and loss.

As the morning wore on, the sun climbed higher, casting long shadows across the land. Opal's hands tightened around the steering wheel, her knuckles pale against the dark leather. She was nearly halfway to Memphis now, but every inch of road seemed to stretch out forever. Time seemed to distort, and with it, the crushing weight of grief seemed to grow heavier.

At one point, Opal pulled over at a gas station just outside of Tremont, Mississippi, to stretch her legs. The heat of the day was already becoming oppressive, and she needed a break from the constant motion. She stepped out of the car and took a deep breath, trying to shake the tightness in her chest. As she walked to the small convenience store, the small-town atmosphere wrapped around her. The old man behind the counter nodded in recognition, though Opal didn't know his name. She found a few agreeable snacks and sat on a bench outside, looking out at the long stretch of highway ahead. The world felt impossibly wide, and for a brief moment, Opal considered turning back—driving all the way back home to Rhinestone, but she knew she couldn't. Her family needed her, and Thomas needed her too, even if he was no longer alive.

The rest of the journey seemed to pass by in a blur. Opal's mind was lost in the sea of memories, the images of Thomas growing up, laughing, and dreaming. Memories of the protest from a few weeks before flashed across her mind. She hoped that Atlas and his friends were safe. She knew in her heart that they would have been at the protests the first week of May. She knew right away that they were resilient and strong. She hoped that she could be strong for whatever lay ahead.

She was anxious to get to her aunt Ruth. Ruth had always been the strong one—the one who had kept the family together through the tough times. By the time Opal crossed into Tennessee, the day was slipping into early afternoon. Memphis lay ahead—its skyline just visible on the horizon, the lights of the city beginning to twinkle in the distance. The funeral would be tomorrow, but the sorrow had already settled into Opal's bones, as though she had been carrying it for years, maybe even her whole life.

The city streets were busier now as Opal navigated through the mazelike roads of Memphis. She was close, so close, to the place that would mark the end of Thomas' story. The funeral would take place in a small church just off the main drag. As Opal turned onto the street where Ruth lived, she saw the familiar house at the end of the block, its porch light burning brightly in the dark. Ruth's house—once a place of warmth and laughter—would now become the epicenter of grief for the entire family. Opal parked her car, the engine's hum fading into the silence of the afternoon. She sat for a moment, gathering herself, before stepping out and making her way toward the door. Inside, Ruth was waiting. And outside, the world, in all its vastness, was waiting for them all.

The grief was still there, just as palpable as the hot, sticky air of the day, but it would pass, Opal knew. It would pass, as everything did. And the road ahead, though heavy with loss, would eventually carry them both into the future—one that, for now, felt so much less certain.

As Opal stepped into the house, she knew this journey would shape her life in ways she couldn't yet understand. The road from Rhinestone to Memphis had been a long one, but it had been only a small part of a much larger journey—one that stretched far beyond the horizon, to places they couldn't see, but would one day have to walk. The house was full of people; some people Opal recognized and others she assumed were friends and neighbors.

The afternoon passed with small talk and plans for the next day. Opal awoke the next morning with a headache and shaking hands. She was never one to fear death or allow herself to be overtaken with outward emotion, but burying a cousin, a childhood friend, was not something she had ever experienced before. This war had brought everyone's worst nightmare to life, but as everyone agreed, it was a beautiful service. Opal helped her aunt and uncle load up the flowers and plants that people had brought to the church in memory of Thomas. She held the folded flag close to her heart and placed his dog tags next to it on her aunt's mantle in her living room where Thomas' picture hung. It was a quiet afternoon filled with food fit to feed an entire army's worth of people. Photographs were passed around and memories were shared. When Opal went to sleep that night, she slept peacefully and awoke early the next morning feeling well rested. Her heart was still broken, but being surrounded by family and new friends had been nice.

The drive back to Rhinestone was uneventful. Opal only stopped once to fill up the car with gas. She took her time taking back country roads with the windows down. The farmlands stretched out for miles on either side of the road and seemed to go on forever. Opal loved walking through the fields of the farm that butted up against the back of her land. She had plans to expand her little garden and maybe get chickens one day, but she kept putting those plans off. What was the point of putting things off though? No one was promised tomorrow, and she had always known that lesson, but it had recently sunk in even more. Maybe she would forge ahead and make some time to do just that.

When she pulled up to her house a few hours later, she had fully committed to building a nice sized chicken coop with a large rectangular shaped run to keep them safe from the dangers of hawks, foxes, and whatever other critters would see the chickens as a tasty meal. Her chickens would not be a meal for anyone, as Opal was a strict vegetarian. They would be living the high life once everything was put in place.

"Maybe I should get ducks, too," Opal mused out loud. "They are messy little critters. Hmm. Something to ponder." She tossed her dirty laundry in the machine and unpacked her small suitcase quickly. She peered out the small window of the kitchen and eyeballed the large side yard that would be perfect for the chickens and saw Maude saunter over from her house.

"What are you up to?" Maude asked warily. She could always tell when Opal had a new project up her sleeve. Somehow she always got roped into helping one way or another with those projects.

Opal grinned broadly and told Maude about her plans for chickens. Maude listened intently and held her questions until Opal was finished.

"Ok, now that you're taking a breath, remember that chickens smell. They smell horrible. And they're loud. And they're messy. And they smell. But aside from all that, are you ok?"

"I am ok," Opal nodded. She hugged Maude tightly and took a deep breath. "I'll give you some of the eggs every day. Think about it, Maude! Fresh eggs daily," Opal smiled.

"I can get fresh eggs at the Pig any day of the week," Maude countered.

"I wouldn't say that exactly," Opal frowned.

"How long 'til we can eat them?" Maude asked.

"The eggs? Whenever you want," Opal explained.

"Not the eggs! When can we eat the chickens?" Maude asked.

"Maude! You aren't eating my babies!" Opal gasped. "How could you say such a thing?"

"Chickens are for eating," Maude said impatiently. "Anyway, I didn't come over here to argue about chickens. How was the drive?"

"It was fine," Opal sighed. "It was good to see everyone again. Service was beautiful."

Maude could tell that Opal didn't want to say anything further about it at the moment, so she relented. "How many chickens are you thinking?"

"Forty," Opal nodded.

"Forty?" sputtered Maude? "Opal Tyler! There ain't no way."

"I'm kidding," Opal smiled softly. "Probably five or six."

"Ok, I can handle five or six," Maude replied. "With forty you'd need a damn chicken house the size of your own house."

"Maybe one day," Opal shrugged.

"You gonna build it yourself?" Maude asked. She somehow already knew the answer to her question.

"I figure between the two of us we can manage," Opal said resolutely.

"If the two of us includes Jameson Montgomery, then maybe," Maude chuckled. Jameson had a knack for building things.

"I just had a brilliant idea," Opal interrupted. "Melanie needs a project for her badge. Maybe she'd like to help!"

"Melly is too much like me when it comes to tools," Maude said. "I don't know if that's the best idea. Lord help her. She gets it honestly from Ruby, too."

"Great idea, Maude! We can make it a group project! I know you had so much fun with all the girls last time. We can all build a coop together," Opal continued.

"Oh dear God," Maude coughed. She wasn't sure how it had become her idea, but she could see that Opal's mind was already made up to involve Melanie's Girl Scout group. "We're definitely going to need Jameson to oversee this thing." She made a mental note to call Ruby as soon as she got back to her house to let her in on Opal's plan. Somehow she knew that Ruby wouldn't be too keen on the idea either.

"This is going to be great!" Opal said.

"It's going to be something," Maude nodded.

Chapter Twenty

The following Saturday morning started bright and early for the assembled crew. Maude begrudgingly shuffled over to Opal's yard where the crowd had gathered for instruction. She was still in her bathrobe, but Ruby could see her pajama pants sticking out underneath the hem of the blue robe. She had shoved her feet in her boots before ambling over. She held her mug of coffee close to her nose to smell the warm steam coming off the brew. She inhaled the steam and suppressed a yawn.

"Don't snort it while it's hot," Opal snickered. She floated between her two friends who were huddled close together a few feet away from the eager group of preteen girls.

Maude rolled her eyes and ignored Opal. She sipped her coffee gingerly and turned towards Ruby who was next to her. "Ruby, why did we agree to this again? And is she seriously barefoot?"

"I don't think we had much of a choice," Ruby yawned. "And when is Opal not barefoot?" She surveyed the sight in front of her. Jameson and another father of one of the girls had organized the lumber into neat piles and made sure the girls were listening before they explained the plan. Ruby had heard it enough times that she had it practically memorized, but at least the girls looked eager to begin. Opal was beside herself with excitement.

"Think they'll notice if we head inside?" Maude whispered.

"I think they're pretty well covered," Ruby nodded. She began backing up towards Maude's house slowly. Maude turned on her heel and rushed to her front door about fifty yards away. "Maude!" Ruby hissed. "I thought we were being secretive!"

"They don't seem to care," Maude shrugged. She sank down into the rocking chair on her porch and yawned loudly. "Maybe I'll just sit right here and rock until I fall asleep. It's too damn early."

Ruby couldn't disagree with that statement. Saturdays were her only days to sleep in, but today she was up before the sun to help Melanie and her group of friends earn their latest badge. Thankfully, Jameson and one of the other dads had agreed to supervise the project, but Ruby still tagged along. Maude yawned loudly and downed the rest of her coffee. "I'm hungry," she mumbled.

"I figured you had already had your breakfast," Ruby chuckled.

"Not yet," Maude replied. "I needed the coffee to fully wake me up. Have you eaten yet?"

"We ate some banana bread before we left home," Ruby nodded. "But I wouldn't say no to something else. What are you thinking?"

"Scrambled eggs and bacon? Grits and toast?" Maude asked.

"What are we waiting for!" Ruby said. She followed Maude inside her house and helped her get out the carton of eggs to scramble. "In a few weeks you will have fresh eggs being so close to Opal's new chicken coop."

"Oh praise the Lord," Maude said sarcastically. "She already told me I can't eat the chickens. What good is a chicken if you can't eat it, Ruby?"

"Opal sees them as pets, not food," Ruby explained. "You know that."

"I know. She's always been an odd one," Maude nodded.

"She isn't odd," Ruby chuckled. "She's unique."

"Always the politician," Maude giggled.

The two friends spent the next little bit cooking and then eating their breakfast. Opal walked in an hour later while Ruby was rinsing the dishes and grinned broadly. "I wondered where you two had run off to! I should have known," she laughed. "Anyway, the coop is looking great. Those little girls know how to use a hammer and nail, I'll tell you what!"

"Oh really?" Maude asked.

"Well, Jameson and Hugh are doing most of the work, but the girls are having a great time!" Opal smiled.

"How are you doing, Opal?" Ruby asked. "I haven't seen you since you got back from Tennessee."

"I'm ok," Opal said slowly. "Just processing. It feels strange to know that I'll never get another letter from him or see him after the war. I got a letter yesterday morning from one of my pen pals, and for a moment I thought that maybe it was all a bad dream, but then I saw the scrawled penmanship and knew that it was from Byron who is recovering from his wounds in Virginia and I realized that I have to continue on. I have people who are counting on me to write them every day and visit them and send those care packages. I can't let the bad things win."

"Well said," Maude agreed.

Ruby set down the dish she had been drying and hugged Opal tightly. "You're a good egg," she smiled.

"Speaking of eggs, Farmer Johnson down the road said he'd bring over a few laying hens when my coop is ready. No roosters," Opal chuckled. "I don't think I could keep him safe from Maude if he wakes her up!"

"Thank God!" Maude exclaimed. "I don't need another thing on this road waking me up any earlier. Between those coyotes who moved into the neighborhood and howl at the moon every other night and the dog who likes to join in, I'm losing out on my beauty sleep!"

Opal laughed out loud and turned it into a cough. "Coyotes?" she asked.

"Opal Tyler!" Ruby giggled, catching onto why Opal was suddenly so tickled. "Those aren't coyotes, are they?"

"What do you mean?" Maude asked.

Opal and Ruby continued to giggle as Maude got more frustrated. "I swear! If that's you coming up to my window howling and getting the dog all bent out of shape, I'm going to whoop you!"

"You couldn't catch me even if you tried and I walked," Opal laughed. "Anyway, I was trying to communicate with nature. You should try it sometime."

"I'll show you how to communicate with nature," Maude grumbled.

"We better go check on the progress," Ruby interrupted. She held the front door open for Opal and Maude who begrudgingly followed Opal back towards her house, grumbling under her breath the whole way.

"Wow!" Ruby exclaimed at the sight of the chicken coop. "This looks amazing!"

The bones of the chicken coop had all been laid out and assembled. The coop held a few nesting boxes and measured three feet by six feet and stood about four feet tall with a perch for the chickens to roost. Attached to the coop was a long run that ran eight feet in front of the coop with a ramp to allow the chickens easier access to the indoor structure. The group had not installed the chicken wire or reinforced the wire yet, but that would not take much time. It was really starting to take shape!

An hour and a half later, with Maude and Ruby's help, the coop was ready to go. Opal could not believe how perfect it looked. She thanked the girls and the beaming fathers for their hard work and passed out sandwiches, chips, and lemonade for them all to have a quick lunch together before the girls all went home. The group of girls were so excited to see that together they had been able to accomplish such an amazing project. Opal promised to invite them back over as soon as the chickens were settled.

Farmer Johnson helped Opal get the six hens settled in early the next afternoon. "Now don't get too upset if they ain't exactly friendly," the old man said gruffly. "They ain't exactly pets. And once they stop laying, just fry 'em up and let me know if you want some more. I got more chickens than Vicky and me know what to do with."

Opal smiled and held her arms out to the nearest chicken who slowly walked over to her. "Oh! Aren't you just the sweetest little thing!" Opal cooed. Farmer Johnson's eyes near about fell out of his sockets as the chicken allowed itself to be snuggled by the cooing woman. "Well, ain't that something!" he echoed. No one was more in tune with animals or nature than Opal Tyler.

True to her word, Opal gathered up the fresh eggs every day and stored them in a basket on her kitchen counter. She enjoyed a breakfast of eggs every morning. Sometimes she scrambled two or three, other days she poached them or served them over easy on a slice of toasted bread. Her garden was also taking shape. The tomato plants had grown and the squash were nearing time to pick. The wild blueberry bushes behind her house were ripe with berries. She picked a few bucketfuls and gave some to Maude and Ruby, then allowed the birds to have their fill of the rest. Ruby made homemade blueberry muffins with some of the wild blueberries and everyone agreed that they were easily the most delicious muffins any of them had ever tasted. Ruby was an excellent baker and fresh ingredients always made things better.

"These are too good, Ruby," Maude said after her third one.

"Thank you," Ruby blushed. She opened her notebook to a blank page and made a few notes after glancing at the calendar on the wall. "School is almost out. The end is in sight!" Ruby loved her job as a teacher, but she'd be lying if she said she didn't look forward to summer break. She enjoyed the few weeks at home with her daughter and always looked forward to their annual summer vacation. Sometimes Maude or Opal tagged along, and sometimes Melanie brought a friend. Often they went to the beach for a week, but Jameson had proposed a trip to the mountains in Tennessee and possibly renting a cabin in nature. Melanie wasn't too keen on that idea. She wanted to go back to the beach and spend a day at Miracle Strip Amusement Park.

"Now that Maude's a wealthy woman, she can take us anywhere in the world. What about Italy?" Opal giggled.

"Nope, No. Never," Maude shook her head. "Italy was once in a lifetime, and I've had enough worldwide adventures for a lifetime. Probably for two lifetimes."

"I agree," Ruby nodded. "That was definitely an adventure of a lifetime."

"What about Florida?" Melanie suggested. "I thought we had decided on Florida. We could all ride the rides and maybe learn to surf."

"Have you ever seen Maude walk a straight line? I haven't either! On second thought, I'd pay good money to see her surf," Opal laughed out loud.

"That would involve me being in water deeper than my knees, so no ma'am," Maude shook her head.

"I could use a tan," Ruby shrugged.

"The salt air is great for a myriad of ailments," Opal announced.

"So we're going for sure going to the beach again?" Maude asked.

"Yay!" Melanie cheered. She pumped her fist in the air and danced around the kitchen. "I love the beach!"

"As long as there is food present, I'm fine wherever we go," Maude nodded.

"We aren't catching our own food," Opal laughed. "Well, we could harvest our own ingredients! Now that's an idea! Seaweed is a wonderful food if you know how to work with it. I bet you'd all love it."

"No!" Maude and Ruby both exclaimed.

"I'm just saying it could be fun," Opal shrugged. "Widen your horizons, expand your palate."

"My palate is already widened or expanded or whatever you said," Maude gagged.

"Suit yourself," Opal frowned. "Just know that I'm prepared in case anything happens."

"If anything happens I'll walk across the street to the hamburger joint and be just fine," Maude chuckled.

There were more than enough restaurants scattered along the beach. They would not have any trouble finding somewhere to eat. The biggest question would be deciding which restaurant to choose during their limited time on vacation. A week at the beach was never enough.

"The Ladies Auxiliary is having that yard sale next weekend. Do you think it's too late to add some more items to the haul? Aunt Willy dropped off a few heaps of clothes for some of my guys over at the VFW, but unless they're into wearing hoop skirts and thigh high boots, I might need to find somewhere else to send these particular donations."

"I think you could absolutely add them to the pile. Nadine has been busy pricing things all week. A few more items won't hurt her," Ruby nodded.

"I think I'm going to bring Daddy's old lawnmower over yonder, too," Maude added. "I don't have the time to fix it. Hell, I don't even know if it can be fixed. Maybe some old man has the time to tinker with it, or else he can sell it for scrap parts. I'm tired of it sitting out back."

"Is that why you haven't been cutting the grass out back? I was hoping it was because you had finally started listening to me about the butterflies," Opal sighed.

"What about the butterflies?" Ruby asked.

"Butterflies love the wildflowers that grow all over the fields," Opal explained. "When those wildflowers get cut, the butterflies have nothing. It's really quite sad. Maude's contributing to the eradication of butterflies."

Maude rolled her eyes and continued to sip her iced tea. "Alright, I have to get back to the garage. Peter Thatcher brought his wife's Cadillac back in.

Susan backed into his pickup three weeks ago and yesterday she hit their mailbox. Some people just don't know how to drive, I tell you what!"

"Well if that ain't the pot calling the kettle black," Opal mused.

"What do you mean by that?" Maude asked.

"I mean you're a hypocrite," Opal laughed. "No mailbox is safe when you're behind the wheel."

"Oh hush. That only happened once or twice," Maude shrugged.

"I believe the count is up to five,' Ruby interjected.

"I'm tired of being ganged up on," Maude laughed. "Now let me get out of here before y'all start in on something else."

"Don't hit Ruby's mailbox on the way out," Opal added. She held her stomach as she giggled. "I better scoot on out, too. I'm going to load up those boxes from aunt Willy and then head over to the VFW and do some haircuts there. If they'll let me. Not many of them want their hair so short anymore."

Ruby hugged her friends goodbye and watched as Maude peeled out of the driveway as Opal laughed hysterically at the sound of burning rubber. Once Opal was safely a good distance behind Maude, Ruby wandered back into the kitchen and began searching through her cookbooks for a recipe for dinner. Jameson had been at the office all morning working on some depositions, and Melanie was at a friend's house. The Manor was quiet once everyone was gone. Ruby often filled the silence by singing praise and worship songs or dancing to the current country music station out of Junction. Conway Twitty, Loretta Lynn, and Charley Pride were some of her favorites. Jameson had gotten her a few vinyl records to play in the living room on the old Victrola when she retired into the living room after dinner and the evening news.

"I bet there will be some records to sift through at the yard sale next weekend," she smiled happily as she hummed along to "Don't It Make My Brown Eyes Blue" by Crystal Gale.

Chapter Twenty-One

Melanie was down to the final few days of school. She had a running countdown on her calendar that hung on her bedroom wall. She was a great student, but she honestly cared more about the social aspects of school than anything else. For some reason, her teacher gave them a math test on that Monday. Didn't she understand that no child cared a lick about anything related to mathematics when the sun shone brilliantly all day while they were locked in the school building? Her only solace was the big x marks she crossed out each day before she went to bed. She was so close that she could taste it!

Ruby had an extra week after the students got out of school to finish her reports, clean her classroom, and tie up all loose ends from the school year. She, too, was counting down the days until summer vacation, even if summer break looked different for teachers than they did most students. Ruby would spend the summer worrying about her students, both new and old, and hoping that she had prepared her class for whatever came next in their academic careers. She would begin planning her lessons and think about how she would organize her classroom when teachers had to report back in August. But before she could worry about any of those things, she had to get through the upcoming yard sale. She had spent the evening before helping Nadine price the last few items. The amount of clothes that have been donated could outfit an entire army. Hopefully, the advertising committee had done their due diligence because Ruby wasn't sure what they were going to do with all of the leftover items that had been donated.

Early that Saturday morning, Jameson packed up Melanie for a fun week with his parents in Mobile. They always took Melanie to their beach house for a few days once school was out. Ruby was thankful that it coincided with the big yard sale. She hated to think of Melanie being bored on her first few days of summer vacation.

The sun beat down on the small town of Rhinestone like it had something to prove. The cracked sidewalks shimmered with heat, and even the magnolia trees drooped like tired debutantes, but inside the cramped entryway of Beaver Crossing Holy Church for the Faithful, things were heating up for a different reason.

"Well, I'll be," Maude muttered, fanning herself with a pie tin. "If Nadine tells me to 'perk up' one more time, I swear I'll dump this whole box of doilies on her perfectly teased bouffant."

Opal snorted from behind a tower of old

encyclopedias. "You say that every week, Maude. And yet, here we are. No doilies, no dumping. And her hair is done perfectly, if I do say so myself."

"Because the Lord has not yet tested me enough to follow through," Maude huffed.

Ruby, ever the peacemaker, slid a plate of lemon bars onto the refreshments table and gave her friends a look. "Let's not turn this yard sale into a spectacle. You know Nadine thrives on chaos. If she sees you riled up, she'll think she's winning. Eat something to keep you quiet." She was still surprised that Maude had agreed to help with the yard sale. While Maude loved a good bargain, sitting in the summer heat with Nadine did not rank high on her list of fun.

"She's not winning," Maude grumbled. "She's just irritatingly persistent."

Across the room, Nadine stood at the helm like General Patton on the battlefield. Dressed in lemon-yellow polyester, complete with matching heels and a brooch shaped like a hummingbird, she barked orders at the women setting up the tables outside on the manicure lawn. "No, no, no, Betty! The records go in the entertainment section, not with the home goods. Who listens to Perry Como while doing the dishes?"

"She's got a point," Opal whispered. "I listen to Perry Como while I should be vacuuming."

"You listen to Perry Como because you think he's dreamy," Maude shot back. Opal didn't deny it.

Ruby sighed and adjusted the bun in her hair. "Come on, ladies. Let's just focus on our part.

We've got the baked goods and the vintage ladies accessories section to manage. That includes hats, handbags, and pearls."

"Pearls," Maude muttered. "The only kind Nadine likes are the fake kind that match her personality."

By eight o'clock sharp, the tables were arranged and the scent of homemade cookies, sun-warmed vinyl, and sunblock drifted through the air like a Southern hymn.

"You'd think the Queen of England herself was comin' to this yard sale," Opal said, adjusting a straw hat on a mannequin head.

"Queen Nadine, maybe," Maude joked. "All hail her polyester majesty."

Just then, Nadine swept by, clipboard in hand. "Ladies! I hope everything is in tip-top shape over here. We've got shoppers pulling in any minute, and we want to make a good impression. We're representing the church, after all."

"God forbid we look like normal people with mildly used pots and pans," Maude said under her breath.

Nadine smiled, the kind of tight-lipped expression that didn't reach her eyes. "Maude, dear, why don't you handle the pricing for the accessory table? I think we all know you have a keen eye for value, though not necessarily style."

Ruby reached out quickly to touch Maude's elbow. "Let me help you, Maude."

"Oh no," Maude said sweetly, eyes narrowing. "I'd love to. Let's start with this handbag here. Looks like something Jackie Kennedy might've owned," Maude huffed. "Before she donated it to the poor," she whispered to Opal.

By the time the first shoppers arrived, the grassy lot in front of the church had transformed into a bustling market. Children ran between the rows of tables, women clutched paper cups of sweet tea, and an old transistor radio played "Me and Bobby McGee" from under a pile of scarves. Everything was going smoothly—until it wasn't.

Maude was adjusting a rack of hats when Nadine shrieked from across the lawn. "WHO put the communion serving tray next to the ashtrays?!"

Heads turned. People stared.

"I did," Maude said, not missing a beat. "Because, Nadine, that's exactly how irony works."

Ruby nearly dropped the basket of crocheted potholders. Opal gasped and covered her mouth with a dainty gloved hand. But the moment passed, and Nadine, to her credit, didn't explode. Instead, she pursed her lips and said, "Of course. How clever, but perhaps next time, let's use our wit for good, shall we?"

"Darlin', I'm trying," Maude said. "But it's hard when I'm surrounded by material."

As the morning wore on, the sun blazed hotter, tempers grew shorter, and Maude's patience wore thinner than the hems of the 1940s dresses she was pricing.

At one point, Nadine tried to reorganize their entire section, claiming the "visual symmetry was off." She moved the accessories display next to the lawn furniture section, insisting the juxtaposition created a certain whimsy that customers were so desperately looking for.

Maude stared at her. "Whimsy? This ain't a Macy's window. It's a church yard sale."

"Well," Nadine sniffed, "some of us believe in putting our best foot forward."

"I'd settle for putting a sock in it," Maude muttered.

Ruby intervened again, giving Maude another lemon bar and shooing Nadine away with a fake emergency about a mislabeled toaster.

Later, Nadine staged a raffle using Lucy's prize-winning lemon chiffon cake without asking permission. Lucy, horrified, whispered to Ruby, "She didn't even ask! That cake took me six hours and two broken mixers."

"Well, she's going to regret that," Ruby said, eyeing Maude, who was now slowly switching the raffle tickets out with blank slips. Maude smiled innocently. "Whoops," she giggled.

Around lunchtime, as storm clouds began to gather over the horizon, Nadine insisted on one final push: a sales pitch through the parking lot sounding like a retired cheerleader from her high school days. "Get your vintage pearls, your pre-loved bags! All for Jesus! Don't be a hag!"

"That woman has lost it," Maude muttered, pulling a tarp over the books.

Then the rain came down suddenly and unforgiving. It soaked tables, swept over the costume jewelry like a tidal wave of glitter, and sent the customers fleeing for cover. But instead of chaos, there was laughter. Ruby, Opal, and even

Maude began grabbing what they could to shield it from the rain. Nadine, hair collapsing like a failed soufflé, ran after a runaway folding chair in her yellow heels, shrieking like a banshee.

Maude doubled over laughing. "Look at her go! That's a new kind of Holy Spirit."

Ruby coughed to cover her chuckle, and Opal held up a broken umbrella like a sword. "Ladies, we've survived worse."

When the storm passed, the yard sale lay in ruins. The accessory table was half-toppled. The hats looked like wet birds. The lemon chiffon cake was mush, but no one was crying. Nadine, soaked but still upright, approached the group. She looked at Maude with what might have been humility or exhaustion. "I suppose this wasn't quite the success we envisioned," she said in a low voice.

Maude, still dripping, handed her a dry towel. "Well, Nadine, maybe not. But the church needed the help, and we showed up. Rain and all."

Nadine blinked. "That's surprisingly gracious of you."

"Don't get used to it," Maude smirked.

Ruby smiled, linking arms with both of them. "We may not have made a fortune, but we made memories and I think that counts for something."

Lucy looked at the soggy remains of her cake. "Amen to that. Though next time, maybe we should put the cake in the church refrigerator."

By mid-afternoon, the sky had cleared and a soft blue hue stretched across the horizon like a quilt. The scent of wet grass lingered in the air as

Ruby, Maude, Opal, and the other ladies cleaned up the tables and tried to dry off what items could be saved. Nadine trashed the soggy cake, much to Maude's fury. Maude was sure that at least some of it could be saved. She trudged up the front steps, still slightly damp and entirely indignant. "I swear on my mother's pecan pie recipe, if Nadine ever comes near another baked good in my vicinity, I'll make sure she ends up in a casserole dish."

Ruby chuckled. "Oh, Maude. She's not that bad. That poor cake had seen better days."

"This isn't so bad either," Opal added, carefully adjusting her new to her handbag, which now contained a soggy bingo flyer, two sets of costume earrings, and a ceramic Jesus figurine. "This thing's a disaster, but I couldn't just leave him there."

Maude peered inside and squinted. "What in heaven's name? Opal, I think that's a toothbrush holder."

"Oh? Is it?" Opal mused. "Well besides, Jesus should be in every bathroom."

Later that evening in Magnolia Manor's living room, the ladies sank into the cushioned chairs like tired queens returning from battle. The window was open just a crack, letting in the lilac-scented breeze and the distant buzz of cicadas. "I still don't know how we didn't kill each other out there," Maude murmured.

"Divine intervention," Ruby said simply, holding out a plate of shortbread cookies she'd stashed for an emergency. "And sugar. Mostly sugar."

They each took a piece, chewing in

companionable silence for a few moments before Opal spoke up again. "Y'all remember Mrs. Winthrop?"

"The one who wore purple wigs and told everyone she used to be a silent film star?" Maude asked.

"That's the one," Opal said. "She always said the best things in life came out of a mess. She called it beauty from the broken."

Ruby smiled. "I remember. She said it the day she tripped and fell into the creek."

"Well, she had a point," Opal said. "Today was a mess, but it was our mess. And we raised some money, even if most of it was in the form of wet nickels and a 1964 Kennedy half-dollar Nadine is convinced will appreciate in value."

Maude rolled her eyes but didn't argue. "Fine. I guess it wasn't a complete waste. How much did we make?"

"A little over two hundred dollars, I think," Opal said.

Maude raised an eyebrow. "Two hundred dollars? That's not bad for a bunch of soggy hymnals and polyester."

Ruby beamed. "That's more than I thought."

Maude sipped her tea. "Still can't believe Nadine didn't demand we do another day of sales."

Opal looked out the window and chuckled. "Don't worry. She'll probably come by any time now with a suggestion for next year's fundraiser."

"Let her," Ruby said. "I for one welcome any productive idea."

About that time, there came a succinct rap on

the front door. Nadine had changed clothes and carried a clipboard with a notebook in one hand and peach cobbler in a glass dish in the other. Maude jumped up to answer the door.

"Oh," Nadine said. "Maude. I didn't expect you."

"Likewise," Maude said.

Nadine held up the cobbler like a peace offering. "Thought I'd drop this by. It's my mama's recipe. Figured I owed y'all something for throwing the lemon cake away. And for being a bit much."

Maude blinked. "A bit?"

"I'm practicing understatement," Nadine muttered. "New thing."

Ruby and Opal appeared behind Maude, surprised to see the rival turned humbled baker. "Well," Ruby said, "come in. We were just talking about the yard sale."

"I promise not to suggest improvements," Nadine said, stepping inside. "Although, I did have one thought about parking."

Maude groaned.

"Joking!" Nadine added quickly, holding up her hands.

They gathered around the dining room table, sharing the cobbler as the setting sunlight warmed the room. For the first time in years, Maude and Nadine weren't exchanging barbs or sideways glances. Maybe it was the sugar, or the relief, or just the passing of another long, messy day, but something had shifted.

"I may have given you a hard time," Nadine said finally. "But truth is, I admire you ladies.

You've got grit and you put up with a lot. Yes, Maude, you all put up with me."

"We all put up with each other," Ruby said kindly.

"Speak for yourself," Maude replied, though the edge in her voice had softened. "You do have good cobbler, I'll give you that."

"High praise," Nadine said with mock solemnity.

A few days later, the Ladies Auxiliary met at Nadine's house for their monthly meeting. Nadine stood at the front of the group and smiled. "I'd like to propose something new," she said. "Next year, we do a themed yard sale. I'm open to any ideas. I'm thinking the bigger the better."

Opal cleared her throat. "Or," Nadine added quickly, "maybe we just keep it simple."

As the meeting wrapped up thirty minutes later, the women filed out into the warm June evening. Ruby lingered with Opal on the porch steps and gazed at the sunset. "Think we'll still be doing this when we're eighty?" Opal asked.

"I plan for you to be leading the charge," Ruby laughed. "With Nadine as your co-chair."

"If she brings cobbler, we'll talk," Opal agreed.

Chapter Twenty-Two

The scent of summer honeysuckle drifted through the open kitchen window of Magnolia Manor, mingling with the faint hum of crickets and the soft clinking of glassware. Ruby stirred a pitcher of sweet tea with the precision of a chemist and the grace of a hostess who'd been setting tables and minds at ease for over decades. It was a sunny Saturday morning, Ruby's first official day of summer vacation, which meant that Maude and Opal were gathering in the familiar kitchen to celebrate. Opal brought a chess pie, and Maude brought her hungry appetite.

"Did you hear?" Maude said as she smoothed her dark-blue shirt, never one to waste time on pleasantries. "They've ratified it. It's official. Eighteen-year-olds can vote now."

Opal raised her eyebrow as she carefully sliced the pie. "Last week they couldn't be trusted with a cup of coffee, and now they're trusted with the country."

Ruby handed around the tea glasses, lemon

wedges perched on the rims like small yellow moons. "I think it's about time," Opal said firmly, crossing her arms. "If they're old enough to be sent to war, they're old enough to have a say in the matter. If they're old enough to fight, they're old enough to vote," Opal nodded again. "If we can ask them to die on foreign soil, then they should at least be able to vote on their own."

"I agree with that," Ruby nodded. They both turned to look at Maude who had been surprisingly quiet during the morning newscast. "I don't disagree," Maude began. "But you both know that there are youngsters here that are about as sharp as mashed potatoes. Bless their hearts."

"No one is denying that," Ruby agreed. "But Opal's right. We are asking a lot from our younger generation."

"When did we get so old?" Maude chuckled. "Once upon a time we were the younger generation. Ed Sullivan is retiring, the President's got a crusade on drugs, and now kids can vote. What a start to summer."

"Time keeps right on moving," Opal grinned. "How lucky are we! You know that age is a privilege. Unfortunately, it is a privilege denied to many."

"Truth is, I remember when we weren't even allowed to vote until we were practically married off," Ruby mused.

"We weren't even allowed to wear slacks, much less vote," Maude muttered, popping a piece of pie into her mouth. "I hated wearing dresses all the time."

Opal laughed loud and sharp. "Maude, I saw you in a dress last Sunday picking up peaches at the Pig."

"I was in disguise," Maude said. "You know when I visit my parents at their church they like to see me dressed up.

Ruby grinned and leaned back in her chair. The sky was a perfect blue, and below them the garden was blooming with roses and marigolds. "I keep thinking about my niece, Amelia. She just turned eighteen. She's marching and writing letters to the editor, and now she'll be voting, too."

"Well, she's always had more moxie than most," Maude said. "You remember last Christmas? Arguing with your brother about the Equal Rights Amendment in front of the ham."

"She's got fire," Opal said. "But maybe that's what this country needs. We can't just be dusting doilies and letting the boys decide everything."

Ruby sipped her tea. "When I was her age, the only thing I voted for was prom queen." They all laughed then, the kind of laughter that came from knowing each other's history, adventures, missteps, and secrets, and still choosing to sit together every week at the same table with the same pitcher of tea.

Opal tilted her head, mischief flashing in her grin. "Well, speaking of emancipation, are y'all still excited for Panama City Beach on Monday?"

Maude groaned and placed her hand dramatically over her heart. "Lord help me, yes. I've already pulled the suitcases from under the bed. And I even bought a new pair of sunglasses.

Big as pie tins."

Ruby raised her eyebrows. "Oh, going Hollywood on us now?"

"I'm going incognito. I don't want anyone from the church seeing me in a bathing suit."

"Oh, please," Opal waved a hand. "You've got better legs than half the girls in those old magazine."

"Well, they're not seventeen anymore," Maude muttered. "So what's our plan? We'll need to stop along the way to get Melanie, right?"

"Yes. The house is far too quiet without her. Jameson and I both agree that we are more than ready for her to come home. She's having the time of her life in Mobile, but I'm so ready to squeeze her."

Maude wiped her fingers on a napkin. "And when we get to the beach, we'll eat shrimp cocktail and pretend we're debutantes again."

Opal cackled. "You mean debutantes who will soon take their teeth out at night?"

Ruby shook her head, chuckling. "Speak for yourself. We are not that old. Thirty is the new twenty."

"We should rent one of those little cottages again one day," Opal mused, eyes dreamy. "You remember the one with the pink door and the lime green shutters? Had a screen porch and a hammock."

"It also had cockroaches the size of kittens," Ruby added.

"But it was ours for the weekend," Maude said, her voice softening.

Opal reached out and patted Ruby's hand. "This trip couldn't come at a better time. I think we need it. Things are changing so fast. The world's bigger than it used to be."

Ruby nodded. "And sometimes lonelier."

"Well," Maude said briskly, "that's what friends are for. To make it all less lonely." They retired to the living room and Ruby turned on the television. The local news station was talking about the weather for the rest of the weekend. A group of teenage boys were playing baseball in the background.

"You reckon those boys even know about the twenty-sixth amendment?" Opal asked, tilting her head.

"They will," Maude said. "When the draft board calls or they fall in love with some activist girl who drags them to the polls."

Ruby finished her tea and set her glass down. "You know what Amelia said to me the other day? She said, 'Aunt Ruby, history doesn't belong to old men in Washington anymore. It belongs to us now.'"

Opal raised her glass in salute. "To Amelia. And all the stubborn, brave girls coming up behind us." They clinked their glasses, the ice shifting like wind chimes.

"And to Panama City Beach," Maude added. "Where I plan to eat some greasy fried food, sleep late, and wear sun hats bigger than umbrellas."

"Don't forget the sunblock this time," Ruby warned.

"I've got some old bottles from last year,"

Maude said proudly.

"Revolutionary," Opal teased.

That evening, after her friends had gone and the shadows had lengthened across the magnolia tree, Ruby sat alone on the porch. The paper was still folded beside her glass, the headline bold: Eighteen-Year-Olds Gain Right to Vote. She traced the words with her fingertip, thinking of her own eighteen-year-old self, wearing saddle shoes and waiting on life to begin. She thought of marches and speeches, of whispered conversations in beauty parlors and church pews, of the quiet revolutions fought with typewriters and casseroles. It wasn't just Amelia's victory. It was theirs, too. All the battles they'd fought quietly, in homes and schools. The right for young women and men to vote. The right to be heard. The right to choose not to go quietly into history.

Ruby smiled, then reached for her pen. She'd write Amelia a letter, she decided. She'd tell her how proud she was. She'd tuck in a few old photographs from their last beach trip—the three of them, arms linked, laughing so hard the camera shook. She'd write that "history belongs to you now, sweetheart, but we're still keeping the porch warm."

The next afternoon, Ruby stood in her bedroom, surveying the suitcase on her bed like a general preparing for battle. Swimsuit? Check. Sunhat? Check. Paperback novel with a brand new cover? Double check.

She ran a hand over the peach colored cotton dress she'd laid out for the drive. She loved the tiny white polka dots splashed across the design. She had worn it to her nephew's graduation last year. Ruby believed in road trip fashion: simple, breathable, and accessorized with a good pair of sunglasses. True to his nature, Jameson was already packed and ready to go early the next morning for his conference. He was sad to miss the annual beach trip, but this was the last conference on the calendar for a few months, so he was looking forward to some rest and relaxation once this particular season of work was over.

Early the next morning, by the time Opal honked from the driveway in her seafoam-green Dodge Dart, Ruby was halfway down the porch steps, dragging her suitcase behind her. Jameson was finishing loading up their car as Maude sleepily hung her head out of the window of Opal's car. "I'm glad I don't have to drive this morning. I'm too tired to function."

"I hope you packed light," Opal called out the window. "Because Maude brought enough for a fortnight in Paris."

Maude's wide-brimmed straw hat rose like a halo in the window. "I brought options," she said dryly. "A lady must be prepared for weather, whimsy, and wanderlust."

"A lady?" Opal cackled. Her flowy flower print dress was a beautiful shade of lavender. "Sure you can't sneak away?" Opal asked Jameson as he hugged Ruby goodbye. "I wish," he smiled. "I know y'all will have the time of your lives."

The drive from Rhinestone to Mobile was peppered with roadside stands offering boiled peanuts, Coca-Cola in glass bottles, and t-shirts that blew in the breeze like flags. As they got closer to Mobile, Maude was sticky with sweat and grateful for Opal's portable fan, which oscillated lamely from the dash like it, too, had grown tired of summer. "So tell me again," Maude said to Opal who was dancing along to the latest tune on the radio. "How much longer? I'm starving."

Maude was practically wasting away by the time they pulled into the driveway of the Montgomery beach house. Jameson's father helped Melanie load her bags in what little trunk space remained of Opal's car. She wedged herself in the back seat next to her mother and they were back on the road again, after they pulled through a fast food joint for lunch. Maude was easily satisfied with a greasy hamburger and fries, which made the rest of the trip much smoother. By the time they crossed into Florida, the flat pinewoods gave way to glimpses of sparkling blue through roadside palm trees. The air smelled of salt, sunscreen, and possibility.

"Look at that water!" Maude gasped, leaning toward the windshield. "It's bluer than I remember. Lord, it's like glass."

They reached the towering condominium with bright pink doors and lime-green shutters still clinging to its cheerful, slightly shabby charm. It had survived storms, seasons, and the recklessness of youth over the years. Opal unlocked the door and let it swing open with a creak. Inside, the air was thick with the faint scent of lemon cleaner and old cedar. Within the hour, they had unpacked, poured glasses of cold ginger ale, and stepped out onto the balcony with their feet up and their hair pinned.

"I feel ten years younger already," Opal sighed.

"Speak for yourself," Maude said. "My knees sound like popcorn. Speaking of popcorn, we should have brought some."

They dined that night at a seafood shack where the fish was fried to perfection and the key lime pie could've brought a grown man to tears. The waiter, a tanned college boy with a peace sign necklace, flirted shamelessly with Opal.

"He called me darlin'," Opal whispered in the parking lot, hand to her heart.

"He called me sunshine," Melanie countered.

Maude lit a cigarette and said, "He called me ma'am. I win."

Back at the cottage, they sat on the porch with their shoes off and the stars thick above the Gulf. The beach whispered behind the dunes, and the world felt like it had softened its edges.

"I saw something on the news last week," Maude said quietly, sipping from a flask she'd pulled from her purse. "A girl in Ohio got arrested for burning her younger brother's draft card. Said she was doing it in honor of her older brother who came home different."

Opal nodded, "They all come home different, if they even come home at all."

The silence that followed was deep but not uncomfortable. It was the kind of silence that came from familiar grief, honored and shared.

"I think that's why I like coming here," Opal continued. "Something about the ocean makes everything feel smaller. The bad things, I mean."

"And the good things bigger," Ruby added.

They sat until the air turned cool and their limbs heavy with the kind of tired that sleep welcomes like an old friend. Ruby and Melanie had one bedroom, and Opal and Maude shared the other one. As long as Opal promised to stay on her side of the bed, all would be well.

The next morning, Opal rose early and took a walk down to the water. The beach was still, the sun just a suggestion on the horizon. She let the surf lap at her ankles and watched the seagulls quarrel overhead. For a moment, the world stood still and everything was perfect.

Back at the cottage, she found Ruby cracking eggs in a bowl and frying bacon barefoot in the kitchen. Maude was playing a mean game of gin with Melanie who couldn't stop giggling at whatever they were chatting about.

"I had a dream I was dancing with Dean Martin," Maude announced, as Opal poured herself a cup of coffee. "And I wasn't even wearing a girdle."

"You're lucky it wasn't Nixon," Ruby chuckled, sliding bacon onto plates.

They spent the day under an umbrella with magazines, radio tunes, and gossip. Ruby read aloud snippets from Cosmopolitan, Maude criticized bikinis with all the authority of someone who still wore a girdle to church, and Opal tried to flirt with the lifeguard until he told her he was nineteen.

"You should be voting," she huffed. "Not

flexing."

That evening, they returned to the seafood shack and ordered the same meal, laughing that they were becoming creatures of habit. But some habits, like friendship and fried grouper, were worth repeating.

After much discussion, Ruby finally agreed to go to Miracle Strip. She couldn't tell who was more excited between Melanie and Maude. "We can go on that devil ride, right?" Melanie asked quietly so Ruby wouldn't overhear.

Maude nodded discreetly. "I think it'll be fun!" If Nadine could survive it, surely she could, too.

The Starliner, The Haunted Castle, and the Ferris Wheel had everyone laughing as the morning went on. Nobody mentioned the infamous devil ride until Ruby was finishing the last bite of her plain hotdog. Maude had already eaten her fill of hotdogs, funnel cakes, and ice cream. "What's next on the agenda?" Maude asked warily.

"I think I'd like to go on that red ride," Melanie said a little too quickly.

"Which red ride?" Ruby asked. "I'm not going on anything that goes upside down."

"Me either!" Maude quickly added.

"I'll go on anything," Opal shrugged.

"I don't know if it goes upside down," Melanie said. "You know the one, aunt Maude. The one you said Ms. Nadine likes."

"Not that devil mouth one!" Ruby huffed. "Maude! You two together are double trouble!"

"We don't even know what it is," Maude countered. "Let's at least go look at it."

Dante's Inferno had a long line, longer than any of the others they had stood in line for, which Opal took as a good sign. It was surely a popular ride worth waiting for. After the ride assistant assured Ruby that it wasn't anything too wild and it certainly did not flip anyone upside down, she agreed to go on it, but it was obvious that she wasn't thrilled by the idea. Melanie opted to ride with Maude, while Opal and Ruby sat behind them. Once the ride began, it was easy to see why everyone at the theme park loved it. It was fast and in the dark seemed even faster. They all had so much fun that they rode it twice more that same afternoon. By the time they got back to the room later that evening, they were all exhausted and too sugared up to want to eat anything for supper. They decided to take a walk down by the water as the stars began to come out over the water. Since it was their last night, they lit sparklers on the beach and made silly wishes. Maude wished for knees that didn't creak, Opal wished for an age-appropriate date, and Ruby wished to remember the laughter, the light, and the way her heart had felt wide open this week. As they packed the cars the next morning, the beach already felt like a memory forming in real time.

"Same time next year?" Opal asked.

"Absolutely," Maude said.

Ruby smiled and took one last look at the shoreline, sunlight glinting on the waves like bits of hope.

Chapter
Twenty-Three

The bell above the door of The Comb Over jingled its familiar little tune as Ruby pushed her way inside, the humidity sticking to her skin like the cling of a too-tight Sunday girdle. The air was thick with hairspray, gossip, and the warm scent of burnt hair. She and Melanie checked in at the counter and then sat down in two of the empty chairs. Melanie picked up the nearest magazine and began reading all about the latest fashion in Hollywood while Ruby waved to Opal who was currently styling Mrs. Picken's bright red hair.

Opal stood behind a vinyl-padded chair with a teasing comb in one hand and a can of hairspray balanced precariously on the edge of the counter. Her hair was pinned high, an architectural marvel held up by prayers and a half-can of hairspray. She looked up from her client and gave Ruby a wide grin.

"Well if it isn't the queen of the garden club herself," Opal chirped, her exaggerated accent dripping Southern charm and sarcasm in equal measure.

"Opal, honey, that's only because you won't take the crown. Don't think I haven't noticed you ducking out of meetings," Ruby replied, opening up her handbag to put her sunglasses inside.

Maude arrived a few minutes later chewing a piece of gum like she was working through a problem in her head. She wore coveralls, stained from the garage where she worked, and a bandana that barely contained her thick brown curls. "I come straight from the shop," Maude announced before either of her friends could tease her. "Didn't even stop to wipe my hands."

Opal rolled her eyes and nodded toward the sinks. "You're lucky I love you, Maude. Go wash those paws before you touch my good magazines." Maude grinned and shuffled off.

Ruby grabbed a magazine from the stack and fanned herself with the folded-back cover. "Have you seen this? Says Walt Disney World is opening up in October. That's just a few months away."

Opal leaned in, suddenly interested. "I heard about that on the radio! Down in Orlando, right? They said it's supposed to be twice the size of the one in California?"

Ruby nodded, her eyes lighting up. "Twice the size and twice the magic, supposedly. Oh, it sounds so fancy. Imagine it!"

Maude returned, wiping her hands on a floral towel. "That place sounds like a fairy tale on sugar water. Think they'd let three Alabama girls in without a chaperone?"

Opal snorted. "They'd be lucky to have us.

We'd charm the mouse ears right off Mickey."

"I'd go just to see a place that clean and bright," Ruby said wistfully. "I bet there's not a speck of red clay in the whole place."

Maude sat beside Ruby and laughed. "Only you would think a theme park whole would be clean. But enough about that. I've got more important news! Don't you want to hear it? I'm going on an adventure tonight."

Opal raised an eyebrow and leaned on her elbow. "Lord, Maude, every time you say that, it ends with us driving out to some field in the middle of the night or some mess like that."

"You're one to talk," Ruby giggled.

"Not this time," Maude said with a grin. "It's good news. I have a date."

That stopped both women mid-movement.

"A what now?" Ruby asked, blinking.

Maude looked positively smug. "A date. With a man. A paying customer came into the garage this morning. He needed his spark plugs checked, so I checked 'em, and we got to talking. Turns out he's a traveling salesman from Montgomery. His name is Hank."

Opal tilted her head and crossed her arms. "Hank, huh? What does he sell?"

"Farm equipment," Maude said proudly. "But he's not pushy about it. He's real polite. Wore a tie, even."

"A tie to a mechanic's shop?" Ruby asked.

"Either he's got class or he's got no sense," Opal mused.

"Maybe both," Ruby offered.

"Either way, he asked if I'd like to get a bite to eat tonight, and I said yes. We're going to The Bluebird Café in Junction at seven o'clock."

Ruby placed a hand over her heart. "That's almost romantic."

Opal clapped her hands. "Look at you, Maude! I was starting to think you were only interested in dating carburetors."

Maude rolled her eyes but couldn't hide her smile. "I still like the smell of grease more than cologne, but I figured it was time I gave someone a chance."

"You gonna wear that outfit?" Opal teased.

Maude scoffed. "No, I was thinking about that green dress I wore to my cousin's wedding last summer. It's clean and doesn't show too much arm."

"I remember that one," Ruby said. "It brings out your eyes. You'll knock him dead."

"You don't think it's too dressy for a place like the Bluebird?" Maude asked nervously.

"Only if he shows up in coveralls," Opal replied. "You're fine. But let me fix your hair before you go. No offense, Maude, but right now it's looking like a bird's nest in a windstorm."

Maude grinned and gave a mock salute. "Yes, ma'am."

As Opal gathered her tools, Ruby turned the conversation back toward dreams and Disney. "I read they're building a whole hotel inside that thing. Like, inside the bubble. Just imagine being somewhere that fancy!"

"Where people can sleep while surrounded by

all that cartoon stuff?" Maude asked.

"We have been to how many countries over the years?" Opal reminded them. "You know I love a good theme park, but I don't know that fancy is the word that comes to mind. Then again, give me a palm tree any day!"

"Exactly. Palm trees, fountains, even a boat ride that goes through a pretend jungle with fake animals. It's like stepping into another world,"

"Lord," Maude said, eyes closing for a moment, "wouldn't that be something? A world without car engines and busted tail lights and my daddy hollerin' about bills. Just peace, music, and food?"

Ruby nodded. "Yes! I bet they have some pretty good food. They say there's a whole land called Tomorrowland, and another called Fantasyland."

"Sounds like someone dropped a dream and it landed in Florida," Opal said softly.

The shop was quiet for a moment, filled only with the hum of the ceiling fan and the soft slosh of water from the shampoo sink as one of the salon assistants, Caroline, washed another customer's hair.

"Maybe we oughta go," Maude said suddenly. "All three of us. We could take a trip down there once it opens. Stay in one of those fancy hotels and eat too much cotton candy."

Opal laughed. "I can't even afford to replace the linoleum in my kitchen, and now you're talking about another vacation to Florida?"

"Why not?" Maude said. "We work hard. Don't we deserve to see something new? Just once?"

Ruby looked at her hands. "I think I'd like that."

"We could save up," Maude continued. "Start now. Put away a little from every paycheck. Doesn't have to be fancy. Just an adventure."

Opal stared at her reflection in the mirror, her eyes softening. "You know what? Count me in."

Ruby raised her hand. "Me too."

Outside, a train whistle blew in the distance, and the crape myrtle trees swayed gently in the afternoon breeze outside the window. Opal brushed through Maude's hair and began to style it for her upcoming date. Melanie sat really still while Caroline trimmed her hair as Ruby sat under the dryer while the salon buzzed around them.

A few hours later, by the time the sun began to dip behind the pines and cast long red shadows over her house, Maude stood in front of her tiny bathroom mirror holding a tube of mascara like it was a loaded weapon. Her hands trembled just enough to make the wand threaten a smudge. She took a breath, braced her elbow against the sink, and focused.

"You can rebuild an engine blindfolded," she muttered. "You can do this."

Maude wasn't used to feeling ultra girly. Most days, she was elbow-deep in axle grease, her hair tied back in a rag, and her nails cut blunt from years of working at her father's garage. But tonight, she wasn't just a grease monkey. She was something else, something hopeful.

The green dress hugged her waist in the right places, flared at the hips, and made her feel like someone out of a department store catalog. Her shoes, low heels, scuffed but clean, clicked on the hardwood as she walked from the bathroom to her narrow kitchen to peek out the window.

Hank's car rolled into the driveway a few minutes later. Maude's stomach dropped like an elevator. "Lord, help me," she whispered, grabbing her purse and stepping outside before she could talk herself out of it.

The Bluebird Café sat on the edge of downtown Junction, its parking lot wrapped around the kind of neon sign that buzzed a little too loud in summer. It was a favorite for locals who couldn't afford the steakhouse in Montgomery but still wanted tablecloths and pie that didn't come from a box.

Hank was polite. He stood when she came back from the ladies' room, complimented her dress without sounding lewd, and laughed at her stories about brake jobs and her latest customer's disastrous attempt to replace his brakes.

"Not many women work in garages," Hank said, sipping his iced tea. "But you carry it well. Confident. I like that."

"I don't think I'd know how to be anything else," Maude replied.

He told her about his travels all over Alabama, to farms from Tuscaloosa to Tallahassee, endless dusty roads, and hotel rooms that all blurred together. "Gets lonely sometimes," he said. "Most salesmen get used to the quiet, but I think I never did. My radio's my best friend." When their waitress brought pecan pie, Hank leaned forward, tapping his fork against his plate. "So what do you do for fun? Besides fix up old trucks?"

"Well," she smiled sheepishly. "My friends and I were just talking today about going down to Florida when that new Disney World place opens."

Hank's eyebrows lifted. "Disney World? The one with the castle and the talking animals?"

"That's the one," Maude said. "It looked like something out of a dream."

He nodded thoughtfully. "You should go. If you like things like that, I mean. I suppose it's mainly for kids, but whatever makes you happy. Life's too short not to see something magical once in a while."

It was such a simple sentence, but it landed heavy in Maude's chest. She didn't usually believe in magic, but maybe, just maybe, she was starting to.

Back at The Comb Over two days later, Maude sat under the old pink dryer chair reading a magazine. She was getting impatient waiting on Opal who seemed to be taking her time. Opal set her other client's silvering blonde with meticulous care and smiled warmly. "Alright, Mrs. Grey, Caroline is going to ring you out at the counter while I go grab a bite to eat."

"About time," Maude grumbled. "Ruby's probably already finished without us."

"No, she isn't," Opal shrugged. "Are you sure we weren't supposed to bring anything?"

"Nope. Ruby said that Jameson had to work late so she and Melanie were wondering if we'd like to come over for supper and play some cards."

Maude beat Opal to Magnolia Manor, mainly because she didn't see fit to follow every traffic law the way that Opal did. She was standing on the porch with Ruby when Opal pulled up a few minutes later.

"Well?" Ruby said, eyes locked with Maude's over baked chicken at the dining room table a few minutes later. "Was he a gentleman or a grease stain in a Sunday hat?"

Maude smiled slyly. "He was nice. Real nice. Talked like he actually cared what I had to say."

"Did he kiss you?" Opal asked, lifting the biscuit to her mouth.

Maude flushed. "Now what kind of girl do you take me for?"

"The kind who deserves a little fun," Ruby said with a wink. She looked over at Melanie who had wide eyes. She wasn't often allowed to hear such grownup talk.

Maude twisted the bracelet she wore on her wrist. "He did kiss me on the cheek, but it was sweet. I don't know where it'll go, but it felt good."

"I swear, I'm gonna cry," Opal said. "This is what I live for. Real-life romance from an old maid."

"Who's an old maid in their thirties?" Maude asked exasperatedly. "I'm just a few months older than you are, might I remind you." They all laughed, the kind of warm, easy laugh that only happened when you were with the people who knew you best. "What's for dessert?"

"Lemon pound cake," Ruby announced. "Melanie whipped it up herself this afternoon."

"Great job," Maude said appreciatively. "After a few slices, I believe me and Melly have a rematch scheduled for gin. She kept whooping me at the beach, but I think I'm ready to make my way back to the victory circle."

"Y'all go on ahead to the living room while I get these dishes and cut the cake," Ruby smiled. She loved how much her closest friends adored her one and only child.

Maude followed Melanie to the living room to begin their rematch, but Opal stayed behind with Ruby. She helped her gather the dishes and began washing them at the sink. "I can get these," Ruby said gently. "You've been on your feet all day, so why don't you go in there with Melanie and Maude."

"I'm fine," Opal said softly. "Sometimes when there's a lot on my mind I just need to relax for a few minutes and do something mindless."

"What's on your mind?" Ruby asked.

"I got some bad news today," Opal revealed. "Do you remember me talking about Theodore? His friends called him Boxy because he, well, you know."

"I remember," Ruby said. "What happened?"

"He died," Opal said. "I guess the pain got too bad. He isn't the first soldier I know who took his own life, and he won't be the last. Something has to change, Ruby. How can the world have something as magical as Disney world and something so awful as war? It doesn't make sense to me. I know the world is full of saints and sinners, but everyone deserves a fair chance, you know. I just don't understand it."

"Me either," Ruby said. She enveloped Opal in

a hug and patted her hair. "I'm sorry to hear about your friend."

Opal wiped her eyes on her sleeve and nodded. "Ruby? Do you remember when I went to the conference in April?"

Ruby nodded. "Are you going to tell me where you really went?"

Opal smiled sheepishly and asked, "I'm not a very convincing liar, am I?"

"We know you went to Washington," Ruby continued.

"How long have you known?" Opal asked.

"The whole damn time," Maude said as she walked in holding her empty tea glass.

"Oh," Opal whispered.

"We're proud of you, you know," Maude said.

"We sure are," Ruby agreed.

"Thanks, Ruby. Thanks, Maude. Let me finish these plates and we'll go watch Melly whoop up on Maude again."

"You know it!" Ruby agreed. "That girl can beat anyone in gin. I don't know where she gets it from." Ruby sliced the lemon cake into slices and plated each slice delicately. "How about you and I play next?"

"Game on," Opal agreed.

Acknowledgments

This book would never have been possible without the love and support of my family and dear friends. To my children, I love you more than you will ever know. Thank you for being the greatest blessings I could ever hope to have.

About the Author

Wanda Jennings writes books about family, lifelong friendships, and the adventures that come with living in a small town! Her books have received starred reviews online and in print, as well as standing ovations and sellout shows during the performance run of Color Me Crazy at Warner Robins Little Theatre. Her first book, Dirty Laundry, received the 2021 Georgia Independent Author Award for Literary Fiction.

Before she started writing comedic fiction, Wanda received a degree in English Literature from Troy University in Alabama. Wanda is represented by Between Friends Publishing, formerly known as Southern Willow Publishing. Wanda loves to cook and enjoys reading poetry on her front porch. When Wanda isn't writing the Magnolia Manor series, she can be found planning her next adventure or in her garden with her honeybees.

Email: magnoliamanorseries@gmail.com
Website: magnoliamanorseries.com
Facebook: facebook.com/MagnoliaManorBookSeries
Instagram: MagnoliaManorSeries

Dear Reader,

I hope you enjoyed Bless Your Heart. I am truly blessed that you took the time to once again spend some time with some of my treasured friends in Rhinestone. Some of you may have even traveled to Rhinestone, or a town just like it, before. If you're like me, you may even be related to a few of these characters yourself!

I am currently working on the next book in the Magnolia Manor series. This next project will be all about Maude, Wilbur, Emily, and the iconic Mavis during a very poignant time in all of their lives. Time & Again which will be available later this year!

Thank you again for supporting this series. The Magnolia Manor series has truly been lifechanging for me in ways that even I could not have predicted. I feel like these characters are real live breathing individuals with histories and futures. It is a privilege to know them so well. I would really appreciate it if you could take a few minutes and leave a positive review on Amazon.com and Goodreads.com. Your feedback is very important to me and it helps spread the word about the series.

Thank you again for humoring me. I have always wanted to share the Rhinestone gang with the world and I am so thankful that I found a way to do it. I look forward to the remaining stories that have yet to be told.

Love,
Wanda

The adventures will continue in Rhinestone this summer. Join your favorite characters as they navigate life's ups and downs in

Time and Again
Available Winter 2025